Readers love
ANDREW GREY

Planting His Dream

"Andrew Grey gives us another good book about finding love and holding on to it despite tremendous odds."

—The Blogger Girls

"Yet again Andrew Grey has managed to capture my imagination by presenting a deceptively simple situation in a light that made it interesting, revealing, and very moving. Bravo!"

—Rainbow Book Reviews

The Lone Rancher

"As with many of Andrew Grey's stories, *The Lone Rancher* is a well written and easy read that leaves you with a HEA."

—The Novel Approach

"This story has an intriguing plot with twists and turns in just about every chapter and was real enough to make it believable… A hot sexy read by the fabulous Andrew Grey."

—Bike Book Reviews

Eyes Only for Me

"Andrew Grey manages to take an emotional rollercoaster of a love story and turn it into a teaching moment."

—Prism Book Alliance

"This is a good story, with well written, well developed characters. There are some seriously hot, steamy scenes, and deeply profound dialogue between the main characters"

—Divine Magazine

By Andrew Grey

Published by
DREAMSPINNER PRESS
www.dreamspinnerpress.com

By ANDREW GREY

Published by
DREAMSPINNER PRESS
www.dreamspinnerpress.com

CHASING THE *Dream*

ANDREW GREY

Published by
DREAMSPINNER PRESS

5032 Capital Circle SW, Suite 2, PMB# 279, Tallahassee, FL 32305-7886 USA
www.dreamspinnerpress.com

Chasing the Dream
© 2016 Andrew Grey.

Cover Art
© 2016 L.C. Chase.
http://www.lcchase.com
Cover content is for illustrative purposes only and any person depicted on the cover is a model.

ISBN: 978-1-63477-470-3
Digital ISBN: 978-1-63477-471-0
Library of Congress Control Number: 2016903149
Published July 2016
v. 1.0

Printed in the United States of America
∞
This paper meets the requirements of
ANSI/NISO Z39.48-1992 (Permanence of Paper).

BA and Julia.
You're fabulous friends and amazing women.
I love you both!

CHAPTER 1

BRIAN PAULSON stood in his living room surrounded by people he knew, holding a martini glass that one of his friends refilled as he passed through the crowd. They'd recently stopped mixing drinks, so all Brian got this time was a splash of gin to resoak his olives. Not that it mattered in the least. He was on top of the world, literally. His condominium near the top of Cudahy Tower was one of the most prestigious addresses in the city, he was surrounded by the crème de la crème of young people in Milwaukee, and he was the center of attention. "Eat, drink, have fun!" he said to no one in particular. That was his motto. Well, most of it. He lived his life on the philosophy that if life was a banquet, he was going to have the biggest, best, and most popular, so "eat, drink, fuck, have fun, and don't worry about anything" was probably more accurate.

A cry went up from the assembled people, and the man who'd come with Peter Gervais wrapped an arm around Brian's neck and pulled him into a deep kiss that dang near curled his toes. "Let's go somewhere for a little of that fun you're so famous for," he tried to say, but the guy was drunk enough that the words were slurred. Besides, Brian didn't even know the guy's name. He was hot enough to meet Brian's standards, but in his liquored state, he doubted the guy could get anything up for more than two seconds.

"How about we get you another drink?" Brian offered.

"Petey," the slobbery guy called as Peter passed by. He dislodged himself from Brian and glommed on to Peter, kissing him sloppily.

1

"If you two want to get it on, go down to your own place," Brian told Peter, who grunted without dislodging himself from the guy and headed toward the door.

"Brian," Simone Lavender said as she sidled up to him. "I know you're gay, honey, but I was talking with Giles over there, and he says you know what you're doing with what you're packing, so I was wondering if you'd like to take a walk on the wild side to see what you've been missing." She normally had a voice that was as smooth as silk, and she never wanted for companionship, but when Simone drank, she sounded huskier than a trucker after a week on the road. She also had the manners of one, which she demonstrated by groping him and giggling. "Damn, honey."

Brian removed her hand and settled her down on the sofa. He handed her his glass and went in search of something else.

"Thanks for the evening," Dennis and Richie said as they half held each other up.

Dennis was an art gallery owner, and Richie had inherited three car dealerships from his father. Brian waved as someone turned up the music, and he began to sway his hips, letting the music take him.

God, he loved having a good time, and it continued even as it grew later and the party settled down. People drifted away, and the group got smaller.

"Hey, Brian, there's some guy on the phone who says he's your uncle," Ryan called from the bar area. He tottered over and pressed Brian's phone into his hand.

"Brian," his uncle snapped. "I hear you're up to your usual." His voice was filled with condemnation, the hypocrite.

"How's the mistress, Uncle Harry?" Brian asked, then covered his mouth. "I guess I wasn't supposed to say anything about that, was I?" He laughed evilly. "Or was that okay as long as Aunt Jean isn't around?"

"Brian," he snapped again.

Dang, he loved getting under the asshole's collar—just part of the fun with his fucked-up family.

"Your grandfather passed away this afternoon."

Uncle Harry was all business, and for a second, the pang that jabbed at Brian's heart and gut drove away the people in the room as well as the music, and all was quiet.

"Did you hear me?"

"Yeah, I did." Slowly the sounds around him returned, and the momentary jolt of loss drained away. How could he lose what he never fucking had in the damned first place? "What do you want me to do about it?"

"The funeral will probably be in a few days, so for God's sake, show up, and be sober. You don't need to embarrass the rest of the family."

"Lord, we can't let that happen," he added snidely.

"Good-bye, Brian, and sober up." His uncle hung up.

Brian placed the phone on the table next to him. He looked around the room, which swam for a second and then steadied. Suddenly he felt sober, which was the very last thing on earth he wanted at this very moment. Brian walked behind the bar area and opened the cabinet, then grabbed the nearest bottle of tequila, a fancy triangular-shaped bottle. He pulled out the stopper, upended the bottle, and gulped down the strong alcohol. Damn, that felt better.

"What happened?" someone asked from behind him.

Brian didn't bother answering. Instead he walked back to the center of the room, hopped up on the sofa, and stood on the cushions.

"Let's have a toast." Brian looked into the bottle and tried to think for a few seconds. Of course he was beyond that at the moment, so very little came. "To my grandfather, Marvin Paulson, the man behind the money that pays for everything. Never around and distant as you were, you're at least the perpetual life of the party." He was about to drink but stopped himself. "Wait, you can't be the life of the party anymore, because you're dead. So rest in peace and leave me to mine." Brian drank again, not noticing or caring if anyone else did. He wanted to forget everything, and the quickest way to do that was through the bottom of the bottle he had in his hand. He sank down onto the sofa and barely registered as the last of his guests left.

BRIAN'S MOUTH was dry and tasted like dirt. He cracked his eyes open and tried to move. Damn, his back ached, and his leg felt wonky. It took him a minute to realize he was lying on his sofa, head buried in a pillow, and that his leg was twisted up in the cushions. He slowly extricated himself and went to stand, instantly wishing he hadn't moved at all.

"Sorry, Mr. Brian, did I wake you? I try not to."

"It's okay, Maria." He groaned and slowly sat up, holding his aching head. He kept his eyes closed.

"You need this," she told him, and Brian cracked his eyes open enough to take the bottle of water she offered. Like manna from heaven, he opened it and drank half, throat burning for a second before the fire was quenched.

Most of the mess from the party had been cleaned up, tucked away in large black bags sitting by the door. The vacuum had been brought out but set aside, unused for now. Brian didn't think he could stand the sound without puking and was grateful she'd been quiet. He managed to stand and shuffled to his bedroom, which was clean and the bed made. He flopped down on it, closing his eyes and letting his hangover do its worst.

He didn't remember closing the door, but Maria must have, and then the muffled hum of the vacuum reached his ears. He grabbed a pillow off the bed and dragged it over his head, waiting for the sound to end.

"Mr. Brian," he heard a few minutes later once it had quieted.

"Yeah?"

"I'm all done," Maria said quietly. "I take out trash."

"Thank you." He reached for the water and drank the rest of it. At least that made him feel better. Slowly he got up off the bed and went into the bathroom, where he took some painkillers and stared at his scraggly face in the mirror. He needed to clean up and get himself presentable, but first he needed more water. He drank a glass and then cleaned up before leaving the room.

"I'm sorry about your grandfather," Maria said from the front door as she got ready to leave.

He wasn't sure what to say. He bit back the sharp comment about his elder relation that was on the tip of his tongue. Instead he merely said thank you to the middle-aged Latino woman and heard the door close behind her. Thank God for her. The place had been cleaned and put back to normal. He lowered himself back onto the straightened and fluffed cushions and pillows of the sofa his interior designer had picked out for him.

Up until that moment, the alcohol had done its job, and he hadn't been able to remember, but now his grandfather's death came rushing back. More than anything he wanted another drink, but that wasn't a good idea. So instead he went in search of his phone. He found it and noticed a number of missed calls and texts. They all seemed to be about the same thing, some sort of family meeting his uncle was trying to call together at four o'clock that day. Brian decided to bite the bullet and actually return his father's call.

"So you *are* alive," his father said when he answered the phone. "I was starting to wonder if the party you were having when your uncle called was going to last all night."

He and his father didn't see eye to eye on very much, especially his father's third wife, Candy, who was a year or two older than Brian. And Brian thought it was common knowledge that he was gay. He hadn't made a secret of it for quite a while. What a family he belonged to.

"I figured I'd call you to see what this family meeting is all about."

"The funeral, of course. It's expected that someone as important as Marv will have a proper sendoff, and the family wants to make sure everyone is on board."

"Yeah, on board with what Uncle Hypocrite wants to do."

"Your Uncle Harry is the head of the family now. At least that's how he sees it, and I doubt you're going to be able to challenge him for that honor any time soon."

"Why do you care? Since Mom died, you've been free of the whole mess, and with what you got from Mom, you're considered quite a catch, apparently."

"I loved your mother," his father said, and Brian paused for a few seconds, hearing genuine emotion from his father for the first time in recent memory. "She and I were happy together, and we had you."

"Then what happened, Dad?" Brian asked. "You remarried, and I was sent away because Debbie, dear wife number two, didn't want children." It rankled that his father wanted the second bimbo wife more than he'd actually wanted him in his life.

"You got the best education possible. That was what was important," his father protested. "We don't need to go over all this again. Things were done, and decisions were made that neither of us is happy about, but it's the way it is. I'm going to the meeting to see what's being planned, and you're welcome to ride along if you like."

"No. I'll get there myself. See you at Uncle Harry's house." He hung up and tossed his phone on the cushions. Then he checked the time. It was nearly two in the afternoon. At least his head was clearing. He had time to shower, change, and get something light to eat before he showed up. If he was lucky, his uncle would serve hors d'oeuvres. That was probably a little much, but after the funeral, Brian fully expected his uncle to break out the champagne, because it was likely he'd end up with all the money and power he'd craved for so many years. Not that Brian really fucking cared. As long as they stayed the hell out of his life, he'd be happy and could go on as usual.

Brian went into the bathroom, undressed, and showered, wishing now he hadn't gotten so drunk that he hadn't asked someone to stay. That way he could work off the agitation that seemed so close to the surface with some hard and heavy fucking. That was what he got for deciding to bury his hurt in alcohol. He needed to be more long-sighted in the future, at least where it came to a good fuck. Once he'd showered, he dried himself and pulled on a pair of boxers. Then he opened his huge closet and walked in to decide what to wear.

He had a myriad of choices from every designer known to man. His shopping trips to New York were legendary. He did a quick walk-through and settled on a pair of nearly black Armani jeans and grinned when he saw the scarlet silk Prada shirt he'd bought last month. If they thought he was going to be as fake somber and act as dour as the rest of them were sure to be, they could kiss his ass.

Brian pulled the shirt off the hanger and held the lush fabric in his hands. His grandmother would have scolded him for that last thought. Without thinking, Brian put the shirt back and got the light blue version. His grandmother had always told him it was his best color. "It brings out your eyes, sweetheart," she'd told him once while they'd been shopping together. And it had stuck with him, like so many of the things she'd said to him. His grandmother had passed away less than a year after his mother had died while in West Africa working to help villagers there. Fucking hell, it seemed that everyone had something or someone who was more important than he was. To his grandfather it was either business or all the charities and foundations he worked with up until his death. To his mom, it was children halfway around the world. To his dad.... Things had been good once, but then chasing tail became more important than he was. Only his grandmother had always been there, and within a year he'd lost his mother and his grandmother.

Brian shook off that crap and put on the shirt. Then he got a belt, choosing a fine leather one. He checked himself in the mirror before slipping his feet into a pair of Italian loafers. After a last look, he went back into the kitchen, pulled out the blender, and mixed up a protein shake that he drank down, thankful his stomach didn't rebel, then got ready to go. He grabbed a leather jacket that cost more than most people's mortgage payments, shrugged into it, and then left the condo and rode the exclusive upper-floor elevator down to the parking garage, where he got into his Porsche. He drove up along Lake Drive with the top down, thankful for the jacket but wanting the fresh lake air, until he pulled up in front of the huge mock-Tudor mansion and turned into the drive to park behind a line of expensive cars that would put a dent in the debt of some small countries.

Getting out of the car, he looked up at the mansion and wondered why in the hell everything about his family was as fake as they were. Nothing had any permanence, and houses, cars, people, all seemed fleeting. Once he'd closed the car door, he pulled his jacket a little tighter and strode up to the door. It opened as he got closer.

"They're in the living room," Mrs. Carson said without smiling. "I'm sorry for your loss, Mr. Brian."

"Thank you," he answered automatically. The one he felt sorry for was her. Mrs. Carson had worked for his grandmother and grandfather for years, and now the nearly sixty-year-old woman was apparently stuck working for his uncle. He smiled at her, remembering how she always had cookies and milk ready for him when he visited his grandparents and never forgot a single Christmas until he went off to college. Each year she always placed some small gift in his hand and then pressed her fingers to her lips so he didn't tell anyone. They were never expensive, but he knew they always came from the heart. Too bad he no longer had one.

"Well, Brian is here, late as usual, so I think we can get started," his uncle said, holding a glass of something clear, probably gin, with a few cubes of ice. "Dad's funeral is scheduled for Friday, and it seems he planned it himself. At least that's what his lawyer said a few hours ago. It's apparently a simple service and interment next to Mom."

Brian took an empty chair as far from his uncle as he could and spent most of the time looking out the windows.

"I was also informed that the reading of the will is to be on Saturday."

"There goes your golf game," Brian said just loud enough for everyone to hear. "What a shame. At least the greens will be safe from your divots for one day."

His uncle ignored him, but Brian saw his hand clench and hoped the damned glass broke.

"We've been asked to be there at ten... sharp."

His uncle glared at him, and Brian turned to look out the window at the sparkling water of Lake Michigan once again. He loved the view. Of course that was probably why his uncle bought the place. Looking one way you could see up the coast to the north, and the other you could see all the way to downtown. It was a unique vantage point because of the shape of the land.

"Are there any questions?" his uncle said louder than necessary. "I do expect some sort of press coverage, so for goodness sake, dress appropriately."

He knew that was directed at him, but Brian didn't even acknowledge it at all. "Is this little meeting over?" he asked.

"You could be more respectful," his aunt Jeanette whispered from next to him. "This is your grandfather you're saying good-bye to."

She always made herself out to be the arbiter of propriety and manners, even with a man half her age sitting next to her, expression as vacant as ever. He was probably wishing for all the world he was pumping iron at the gym or something, at least from the way he kept watching himself in the mirror across the room.

"And you could act your age," he whispered back. "But then again, you must have looked a long time to find someone on your intellectual level." Brian had decided some time ago that he wasn't going to take his family's crap. They were all pretty messed up.

"All right, then…," his uncle said, and Brian looked at his watch.

What a total waste of time. Uncle Harry always tried to make himself out to be something important and had to be the center of attention.

"We'll gather on Friday to say good-bye to our father and grandfather."

How his uncle kept the threatening grin off his face was a miracle as far as Brian could see.

The rest of his relatives began to mill and talk. Brian wasn't interested in spending any more time with his relatives than he absolutely had to, so he left the room, heading back toward the door.

"Good-bye, Mr. Brian," Mrs. Carson said as he passed her.

"Don't let any of them get to you," he told her.

She smiled that same indulgent smile he remembered from when he was a kid. "None of them bother me. I'm only here because your uncle asked me to help during the funeral. After that I'm going to retire. Your grandfather and grandmother saw to it that I'd be able to do that." She took his hand. "Now that my time with your family is nearly over, I can say what I've wanted to say for a long time. Your grandparents thought more of you than you know, and they both loved you very much."

Brian had no doubt about his grandmother's love. "He had a lousy way of showing it." Still, Brian appreciated that she cared enough to say something. He leaned forward, kissing her on the cheek. "But thank you." He squeezed her hand and left, getting in his car and driving away from the house as fast as he dared.

He wasn't interested in going home and had no particular place to be. He went back in the direction of downtown and parked outside one of the entrances to Lake Park. This was where he liked to come to think. He locked the car and pocketed his keys. The sun had come out full force, and the wind had died away, so he left his jacket in the backseat and decided to walk for a little while. The park was full of paths, lawns, and glades. It had been designed by Frederick Law Olmstead, the man who designed Central Park in New York, so it had some similar features, including bridges, a lighthouse, sculptural lions, and massive specimen trees. Parts of the park were magical, and Brian headed toward one of the areas with an amazing bridge that afforded a commanding view of the lake.

He walked halfway across, past the stone seating area and the huge lions, onto the bridge, and stood in the middle, staring out at the water. People passed around and behind him as they walked, but he paid them little attention. It had been a shitty day on top of a crappy night, and the rest of the week wasn't going to get any better.

His phone interrupted the beginning of his downward thought spiral. "Hey, Bri-Bri, it's Peter. Do you want to go get some dinner and then take in a club?" He paused a second. "Oh shit, I forgot about your grandfather. I should…."

"No. I'd like to go out." At least it would give him something to do and think about other than his stupid family.

"What are you doing?" a man called in a rather high-pitched voice.

Brian turned and saw a man racing full bore in his direction.

"Stop him, please," another man called.

"What's going—" he heard Peter say and then dropped his phone as the guy barreled into him. Brian prevented himself from falling hard by grabbing the guy and taking him down with him, using him as a cushion. Brian recovered quickly, but the guy who'd been on the run wasn't as fast, remaining still as a small man raced up to them.

"Bastard!" he yelled at the fallen man and grabbed what he was still clutching in his hands. "Steal my wallet." The small guy kicked the other one and looked about to beat him half to death.

"Hey, man," the fallen guy slurred.

Brian grabbed the little man's arm. "Leave something for the police." He found his phone on the bridge decking and made a call. The guy on the ground started to get up. "I wouldn't do that if I were you, or I'll let him at you again, and I think he's ready to kick your ass into next week."

"What?"

He looked at Brian. The man was stoned out of his mind. Brian was well aware of what that looked like. The police arrived on foot, racing up and taking charge of the situation. They quickly ascertained who the real victim was and hauled the stoner off toward a police car.

"Thank you," the small man said, and Brian noticed his huge blue eyes and medium-length blond curls. He could probably use a haircut, but he was cute nonetheless.

"You're welcome, tiger," Brian said with amusement.

"He tried to take all I have for the next week, and if he'd gotten away…. Sorry, you don't need to know that. I'm Cade McAllister, and I might have gotten a little carried away," he said, running at a mile a minute. "That tends to happen a lot, especially when I get excited."

"I'm glad I could help." Brian found himself smiling without thinking about it. Cade had this energy that seemed to spread in all directions. "I'm Brian, by the way," he added, remembering his manners and extending his hand.

Cade shook it and then turned anxiously toward the police officers. "Do you think I can go? Today is my first day of work at Bartolome's, and if I'm late…." He almost danced from foot to foot as he checked his watch. "I left extra time, but I only have a few minutes now."

One of the police officers came over and took Cade aside. After a few minutes, Cade raced back.

"I gotta go, but thank you again, and if you eat at Bartolome's, ask for me, and I'll make sure you're taken care of."

Cade hurried away, almost running along the path. Brian watched him go, wondering how anyone could have that kind of energy and spirit after being mugged. Then, once he was sure the police were done with him, Brian decided spending more time in the park probably wasn't a good idea, even though he had no idea what he was going to do for the rest of the day. He figured he'd call Peter back and go clubbing.

CHAPTER 2

THE FUNERAL had been as awful and depressing as he'd expected. His father had insisted he sit with him and his third wife, Candy. Her name was Candice, and his father actually called her Candy. He did as his father asked for the sake of appearances and to avoid a fight. They were supposed to be one big happy family, after all. Jesus, he should have brought a date. That would have shaken everything and everyone up, but dammit, no one had wanted to attend a funeral with him.

Finally the service was over and so was the graveside thing, which was wet as hell. More than once Brian had looked up at the gray sky knowing his grandfather would be happy. One last thing and that would be it: the reading of the damned will tomorrow. He wasn't expecting anything, and that was for the best—he didn't want anything from his grandfather, at least not now. What he'd needed from him hadn't been given, and he had little use for him now that he was dead.

BRIAN PURPOSELY showed up five minutes late. His entire family was gathered around a huge polished mahogany conference table with a stately older woman sitting at the one end. He figured she was holding the place for his grandfather's lawyer. At a nod from her, the room quieted, and the doors were closed. Two other people from the firm took the empty chairs next to her.

"I'm Lydia Maxwell, Marvin Paulson's attorney and the executor of his estate."

That one sentence explained a lot. He'd seen the Maxwell name on the firm letterhead. Well, that was a surprise.

"I knew Marvin well, and we worked together for many years. I feel his loss professionally as well as personally. He and I were colleagues as well as friends."

Brian stood in one of the corners in the back. He thought of tugging one of Uncle Harry's brats out of a chair so he could take it, but he figured standing out of sight would allow him to make a quick exit.

"Are you ready to get started?" Uncle Harry asked impatiently. He could never wait for anyone else.

Lydia opened a folder. "Marv specified that the will be read. It's in his own words because he wanted all of you to know these are his specific wishes. I will dispense with the legal formality sections and come right to the points of interest. 'To my son, Harry Paulson.'" She paused and looked at Brian's uncle. "I leave my majority share in the Milwaukee Sea Captains hockey team. You were always a sports fan and spent more time in front of the television or out on the golf course than you did anywhere else, so this should be right up your alley." She paused and raised her eyebrows. "It is estimated at nearly twenty million dollars."

"That's it?" Uncle Harry growled, slapping his hands flat on the table.

"Yes. You may leave the room," Lydia said.

"I want to know what everyone else gets," he said, glaring around the table.

"Those were your father's wishes. Once you've received your bequest, you are to leave." She folded her hands over the folder and calmly stared at him. "I can go no further, and your father did make an additional provision. He insisted that I was authorized to have you removed, forcibly, if necessary."

The other two members of her staff added their glares, and Uncle Harry got to his feet and then left. The drama was mildly interesting. His uncle loved to bluster and put on a show.

"To my daughter, Jeanette. Jean, I leave you my interest in Paulson Brothers Brewery. You spent much of your life drinking and spent way too much money because of it. However, since you never had a head for business, control of the company will remain under the board of directors."

"A brewery," she sneered. "How much is that worth? And how soon can I sell it?"

"You can't unless the board agrees," Mrs. Maxwell said levelly. "Good day."

Once again she waited, and Brian's aunt left. Other family members got small bequests, including trust funds of various sizes for the various younger grandchildren.

Finally only Brian, his dad, and Candy were left in the room.

"To my son-in-law, Jerry Northway."

Brian's mother had kept her own name, and when Brian was born, his grandfather had insisted Brian be a Paulson. His father perked right up, but not nearly as much as Candy did.

"I know you loved my daughter, and her loss was a blow to both of us. However, since her death, you have shown very questionable taste in companionship. Therefore, I leave you the house in Shorewood where you currently live, as well as a managed trust large enough for its upkeep that will last as long as you live and is not transferrable to anyone else." Meaning his grandfather had cut Candy out of everything, as well as any future wives. "Beyond that, I suggest you man up and get a job."

His father seemed resigned, but Candy was livid and seemed about ready to explode at any minute.

The three of them got up to leave the room. Brian wondered what was to be done with the rest of his grandfather's money. There was certainly more. But then again, maybe his grandfather had given most of it away within his lifetime.

"I need to get out of here," Candy said snippily, grabbing his father's arm. "We need to find you a high-paying job of some sort, because…."

Brian tuned out her cloying voice, and when a nearly full elevator car arrived, he stepped back and let them get on. Spending any more time around her was more than he could take. He supposed Candy could have been a good person, even a nice person, if she'd taken a more conventional path in life and hadn't hung her hopes and dreams on Brian's father's financial prospects.

The elevator doors closed, leaving Brian standing in the corridor.

"Mr. Paulson," a young woman dressed in a lawyerly gray business suit said. "Please come with me."

"There's nothing for me."

"How do you know, Brian?" Mrs. Maxwell said from her chair in the other room.

He wondered for a second how she knew who he was, but then she'd known everyone in the room earlier, so it was probably her business to know the people in his grandfather's family. He followed the younger woman, and she closed the door behind them.

"This is Emily Forester, and she is fully briefed on all the clauses and stipulations in your grandfather's will."

"What do you want with me?" Brian asked.

"I'm going to let Marv speak to that."

Lydia motioned to Emily, who handed her a large manila envelope that had been sealed with red wax.

"You see that the seal is intact. This was affixed by Marv in our presence."

She opened the envelope, pulled out a memory stick, and handed it to Emily, who placed it into a laptop. The huge flat-screen monitor on the wall came to life, his grandfather's face front and center.

Brian was taken aback at first at how old he seemed. The truth was that he hadn't spent a great deal of time with him over the last few years. "When was this taken?" Brian asked, looking at the still image.

"The will was executed almost a year ago," Lydia answered and motioned to Emily.

"Brian, if you're watching this, then we both know what happened, and you're in the large conference room with Lydia Maxwell and one of her partners. And I'm here to talk to you about your inheritance."

"What inheritance? I don't want anything from you," Brian said.

"You may say you don't want anything, but I know you did. I'm not perfect, Brian, and I've made plenty of mistakes in my life. After we lost your mother, your grandmother and I thought our hearts would shrivel up and die. Then I lost your grandmother, and I think my heart did just that. I know it's no excuse and that I should have been there for you, and I wasn't."

"Yeah, you weren't." Brian turned to Lydia. "This is bullshit. If he wants some sort of absolution, he can go to hell. I'm out of here."

Brian stood and headed for the door. Lydia met him with a hand gently placed on his shoulder.

"Sit back down and listen to the rest of the message," she said with a quiet strength that had him moving back to the chair.

"I can't make up for what happened, but know this. Your mother was the best and brightest hope for our family, and when she died, so did her light. I'm hoping she passed on some of that light to you. Up until now, you haven't been given a chance to demonstrate that, but we'll see. As part of my will, I have set up a number of lessons that I need to know you have learned. They will be explained by Lydia when she feels the time is right, and she will also be the sole judge of completion. So you will want to get on her good side. If you fail, it's over, and you walk away."

The screen went blank, and Brian turned to the lawyer.

"That's it?"

"For now. I want you to meet me in this room at eight o'clock Monday morning, and I will explain the first step in your journey."

18

She stood and extended her hand. Once Brian shook it, she stepped back, and Brian opened the door to the conference room, completely confused but not willing to let it show. Without another word, he left the office and called the elevator.

THAT EVENING he stayed home. However, Sunday morning the phone calls started. "What did you get?" Peter, his first caller of the day, asked.

"I'm not sure," Brian said honestly. "It's a little confusing. But I was thinking that we should get together for dinner."

"Are we celebrating or commiserating?" Peter asked.

"Maybe a little of both."

"Excellent. I'll get a good table at Bartolome's and call the rest of the group to join us. We can't have you wallowing in a sea of unknowns all alone, can we?"

Peter talked a few more minutes and then hung up, probably to get the phone lines sizzling with news and dinner invitations. The rest of the calls were much the same, and Brian ignored them after a while. He didn't want to talk about what he did or didn't get. His head ached, and he was trying to put all this together. Brian figured he'd find out on Monday, and there was nothing he could do about it until then.

Brian kept a low profile until it was time to get ready for dinner. He dressed in plenty of time and took the elevator down to his car, roaring the engine as he zoomed out of the parking garage, swerving to keep from hitting a black van. He grinned and kept going, turning onto Lake Drive and riding out to the fancy restaurant situated on the bluff overlooking Lake Michigan. The setting and the building were gorgeous, and Brian walked in as though he owned the place. He practically did, with all the money he spent there.

"Mr. Paulson, good evening. Some of your party has arrived."

"Excellent, Sandy," he said, and something jarred in his memory. "I was wondering if Cade was working this evening."

"I can find out for you," she said as they approached the best table in the house, with a breathtaking view down to and over the water. Brian took his place at the head of the table without thinking about it.

"Peter said you needed cheering up," Simone said from where she sat next to her husband, Giles, to his right. "Speak of the devil," she said as Peter joined them with a very young and rather uncomfortable-looking man on his arm. He must have been trying to impress the guy.

"This is Brad," he said without offering any other details.

At least Peter was gentlemanly enough to show him to his seat. They talked quietly while the others arrived. Within a half hour, they were ten.

"Brian," Cade said as he approached the table, smiling brightly.

"Good evening, Cade. Please bring two bottles of Dom Pérignon and ten glasses."

He met his smile, and Cade turned, hurrying away.

"You know him?" Peter asked with a raised eyebrow. "Where would you have met him?"

The raised eyebrow and the leer told Brian exactly how far down the gutter Peter's mind was traveling.

"I helped him in the park a few days ago," he explained without offering details, then asked Simone about one of her various charity drives.

Once Cade brought the drinks, they began the dinner that lasted until well after dark, with appetizers, salads, entrées, dessert, all with various bottles of wine. Friend after friend said good night, and Brian pushed his half-full wineglass away. He placed his black credit card in the check holder and handed it to Cade.

"Good night, Peter," Brian said, standing up to hug his friend good-bye.

"Mr. Paulson?" Cade said, and he turned to see him with the manager of the restaurant right behind him.

"There's seems to be a problem with your card," the manager explained.

Brian pulled out his wallet and handed them another.

"I'll have to call them tomorrow."

He turned back to Peter, who said good night. Brad also said good night and followed Peter out. Brian sat in his chair once again, and this time Cade and the manager returned, both looking just as dour.

"I'm afraid this one has been declined as well."

He placed the card on the table, and Brian went cold.

"There has to be some mistake."

"Quite possibly, I'm sure." The manager was clearly uncomfortable.

"You know who I am?" Brian said, holding himself high in order to hide his embarrassment. Nothing like this had ever happened to him. He'd need to call his trustee as well as the bank and yell at all of them in the morning.

"Yes, I do." He sounded snooty, as though Brian had been caught stealing. "Cade is off shift and has agreed to go home with you to get the bill paid. A check will suffice, but if it isn't good, we will call the police, and we will know where you can be found."

Brian wanted to snap at him and put him in his place, but the realization hit him that he was in no position to bargain. The manager could simply call the police, and then that story would hit the papers. His family would have a cow. His fucking aunt and uncle would be making snide comments about it for years.

"Of course. It's just some mix-up." Brian stood to get ready to leave.

"I'll need a minute to change," Cade said and hurried away.

Brian left the dining room. This was one time he did not want to be the center of attention. When Cade came out, they walked to his car.

"I'm sorry about all this," Brian said as embarrassment rose once again. He hated being out of control, and this was certainly that. He had a trust fund set up by his grandfather that was his source of money. He never gave it any thought and never asked anyone else for anything. Being beholden to any of his relatives was not something he was the least bit interested in.

Brian started the car and drove sedately through town, then parked in front of his building. He figured he'd have to take Cade back to the restaurant once he'd straightened this out. They got out of the car and went inside, rode up to his floor in the elevator and unlocked his condo door.

Inside he went right to his desk.

"This is amazing," Cade said, walking over to the windows to peer out.

Brian found his checkbook and wrote a check that included the amount for the bill plus a generous tip for Cade, especially considering the trouble he'd gone through. "Here you are," he said, walking to where Cade stared. He'd seen that view so many times he rarely paid any attention to it any longer.

Cade took the check and put it carefully into his pocket. "I bet you have a front-row seat for the fireworks from up here," Cade said, practically pressing his nose to the glass. He seemed so enthralled that Brian stood next to him, looking down to the park near the art museum.

"I don't think I've ever been here for that." His uncle always had one of his family "command performance" parties at his house.

"What a shame," Cade said softly and then seemed to blink out of his thoughts.

"I should get you back to the restaurant." Brian was anxious to have this whole episode behind him, even if being with Cade was rather nice. There were no expectations, either good or bad. His family always expected the worst, and he usually delivered on that. His friends expected either the clown or the party animal, and he was adept at playing both those roles.

"Yeah." He didn't turn right away. "I love the art museum under all the lights. They have the brise-soleil up, and it looks like it's going to sail away into the night."

Cade practically bounced, and Brian turned to where he was looking. He'd never really paid any attention before.

"It does," he agreed. Brian stood at his own windows for a few more minutes as Cade marveled over what Brian saw every day. It was like experiencing something brand new, and he'd lived here for over a year.

"I'm sorry. I got carried away," Cade said as he stepped back from the window. "I shouldn't take up any more of your time." He patted his pocket. "I appreciate you giving me the check. My boss will be happy about that." The nervous energy seemed to be back once again.

"Let me give you a ride," Brian offered, and they left the condo and rode back down. When Brian stepped outside the building, he instantly noticed a number of things. His car was sitting on a towing company flatbed, and large men moved to stand behind him. "What the hell is going on?"

"The people who own the car as well as the condo have decided that you don't get to use them any longer," one of the men said as he crossed his bulging arms over his thick chest and stared blankly ahead, as though he wasn't even seeing Brian at all.

Brian walked up to the huge man who spoke to him. "I own the condo and the car," he snapped.

"Do you?" he asked and placed a card in Brian's hand. It had his grandfather's name on it and nothing else.

"Shit!" He crumpled the card and tossed it back at the man. "What the hell am I supposed to do now?" Brian yanked out his phone. "Peter, thank God," he began as soon as the call was answered. "Everything is messed up right now, and I need a favor. Can I crash with you tonight?"

Peter hesitated. He sounded winded. "Umm, I have company already. I don't think that's a particularly good idea. What happened? Why can't you stay at your place?"

"My grandfather," Brian answered.

"Is that what happened with the bill at the restaurant?" Peter asked, and Brian wondered how word could possibly have gotten around so fast. "Carolyn Langdon was at the next table. I'm surprised you didn't notice her. She spread the word that you were having money trouble within seconds." Peter groaned softly and tried to muffle it but failed. "I need to go. Call me when all of this is straightened out." He hung up.

Brian wanted to smash his phone on the sidewalk, but he needed it.

"Simone," he said when his second call was answered. "I need a place to crash for a few days. Things are really getting weird, and I need some help."

"Sorry, sweetheart, but we're getting ready to go out of town for a few weeks."

She sounded like talking to him was the last thing she wanted to be doing. What the fuck was wrong with these people? He'd shown them a good time for years. Hell, just a few hours ago he was buying them dinner and having a great time.

"We heard what happened, and I'm so sorry to hear that. If we'd have known, we certainly could have helped, but…. Just a second. No. Don't pack that. I'll be there in a minute. I really need to go. But I'll call you when we get back, and I really hope you get all this straightened out."

She made a kiss noise and then hung up. Brian was floored. Two of his closest friends had turned him away.

Cade had moved out of the way and was on the phone. "Yes, I have the check. Would it be okay if I brought it in tomorrow when I come to work?" Cade seemed nervous once again. "Thank you. I'll come in a little early so you'll have it."

He hung up, and Brian heard a sigh of relief.

24

Brian made a few more calls, none of which were answered, and he left messages with each of them. He told himself he could straighten all this out when he went to the lawyer's in the morning. In the meantime, it was getting late, and he needed a place to stay. He almost called his uncle, but his finger hovered above the number. He hated to ask that piece of work for anything. He shivered both from cold and what his uncle would say.

The night air was starting to get under his shirt. The wind off the lake had died down, but the breeze was still chill and damp. Brian pulled out his wallet to see what cash he had on him and realized there wasn't enough for even a cheap hotel room. He never carried much cash. He always paid by credit card.

"I don't know what's going on, but you can come home with me for the night," Cade offered in a rather quiet voice. "My apartment is really small, and it's nothing like that one." Cade looked up the building. "But I have a sofa you can use for the night." Cade bit his lower lip slightly.

"Thank you," Brian said through his desperation. He couldn't believe his friends had deserted him. All he was asking for was a place to sleep for a single night. That was all the time he needed to straighten this out. "You don't have to do that," Brian said, feeling something he couldn't ever remember, humility.

"In the park, you helped me."

Brian turned to the men by the door of the building, letting others in. He wanted to scream at them again. That was his home. Hell, he thought of calling the police, but if his grandfather had something to do with this, even dead, it wasn't likely they would intervene.

"We need to go," Cade said.

"How do we get to your place?"

"Walk," Cade said and began down the sidewalk.

Brian grumbled under his breath and followed. It wasn't like he had much choice in the matter. He wished he hadn't left his leather jacket in the back of the car. The evening air was cooling by the minute, and Brian's clothes were meant for show, not for warmth.

Cade walked at a brisk pace, and Brian did his best to keep up. His feet ached after a number of blocks, and the moisture in the air increased. If they didn't arrive soon, they were going to get very wet. The air smelled of moisture, and it clung to his skin, making him even colder and more uncomfortable.

"Are we close?" Brian asked one last time.

"Just another block," Cade told him and walked faster.

By the time Cade stopped and headed up a set of stairs, unlocking the door to an old building, Brian swore they had walked for miles. Cade led him inside, and as the door closed, the wind rattled it, followed by a driving rain. "That was close."

Cade climbed three sets of stairs before unlocking a door at the back of the building. Brian stepped inside and was almost totally shocked. The apartment was meticulously clean, maybe cleaner than his, but the furniture was all old, and nothing matched. Against the far wall, a set of shelves had been set up, made out of boards, bricks, and glass blocks. That held the sound system and a small television. The rug on the floor was slightly frayed, and the chair had been draped with a blanket.

"Do you need something to drink?"

"Some water would be nice," Brian answered.

He stood still. He wasn't sure if he should sit down or not. Cade returned with a glass of tap water containing a few ice cubes. Brian blinked and realized he'd been expecting the European bottled water he and his friends always drank. They never had water from the tap.

"Thanks," he said automatically and took the seat Cade indicated.

He was so uncomfortable he couldn't put it into words. All his life he'd been surrounded by luxuries and the best money could buy. This apartment was like being in a strange country where he didn't seem to speak the language. It was in his same city and maybe a mile from his home, but it seemed light years away from where he'd started out just a few hours earlier.

"I have to get up really early, so I'm going to get you some blankets for the sofa."

"I'm supposed to be downtown by eight," Brian said.

"The easiest way to get there is by bus. There's one that stops at the end of the block, and it will take you to Wisconsin Avenue." Cade left the room and returned with blankets and a slip of paper that he pressed into Brian's hand. "This pass has one ride day left, so you can use it all day tomorrow. I also brought you a pair of shorts and a T-shirt. I put out a washcloth and towel for you in the bathroom. Yours are the blue ones."

"Is the restaurant open in the morning?" Brian was never up that early.

"No. I wait tables in the evening, and I get some hours at a health club downtown in the mornings." Cade set down the stack of blankets and clothes on the arm of the sofa. Then he locked the door and pulled the curtains closed. "I'll wake you up in the morning so you have enough time to catch the bus."

He left the small room, and Brian stared at the pile of belongings that would make up his bed for the night. After doing his best to make the bed, he used the bathroom when Cade was done and then changed clothes and curled up under the blankets as the room grew colder, and rain continued to lash the windows.

Brian turned out the light next to the sofa, plunging the room into darkness. Of course he didn't sleep for hours, staring up at the ceiling with its thin cracks and a darker spot in the corner that grew evident once his eyes adjusted. How in the hell had he gone from living in the lap of luxury to cowering and curling into a ball under itchy blankets in a cold room that was completely strange? In his life, rooms were always comfortable in winter or summer. He was rarely cold in winter or sweated in the summer, unless he was outside for some reason. Brian always had everything he wanted, at least materially, but now, under some device, that had been taken away.

Well, he'd see about that. Brian's fortitude showed up after a few hours, and he determined he was going to fight whoever was doing this. If it was his grandfather and some twisted game he was playing with his will, then he was going to tell them all where they could go and what they could do with it. Grandpa Marv hadn't cared enough when Brian had been cast aside as a teenager, so why should Brian give him any effort now? He'd been serious— he didn't want anything from his grandfather other than to have the heartless bastard leave him alone, in life or from beyond the damned grave.

CHAPTER 3

THE FOLLOWING morning, Brian charged into the lawyer's office. He'd slept very little and had actually taken the bus. The only good thing had been the gentle way Cade had woken him. Brian had liked it but wasn't sure what it meant, if anything. Cade had shared his breakfast with him and then made sure Brian got out of the apartment and was on his way in plenty of time.

"Go into the conference room and sit down, Brian," Lydia said as soon as she saw him. She seemed amused by his anger. "There's some juice and bagels if you're hungry."

He went in, grabbed a bottle of orange juice, and drank half of it, ignoring the rest of the food. He sat but held on to his anger. "What the hell is going on?" he asked when she came inside with Emily and closed the door.

Lydia didn't answer. She simply handed Emily another memory stick. Brian sat back, and sure enough, another message from his grandfather began to play.

"Brian, you've always had everything, at least all that money could buy, so it has no value to you at all. I'm sure you're still throwing extravagant parties without thought."

He nodded before he could think about it.

"That has to come to an end. Someone had to earn that money. It didn't just fall into your lap like a snowflake in winter. That money you so callously spend represents someone's hard work and sweat, so that's what you're going to do." The screen was paused.

"What's all this about?"

29

"Brian, your condo as well as your car are the property of your trust, which your grandfather set up, and as of now, all those assets have been frozen. You cannot access any of them."

"So where am I supposed to live? How do I get around?"

"That's up to you." She sat down and passed him a colorful piece of paper. "That is a bus pass. It's good for the next month. Your restaurant bill from last night will be paid. The money to cover the check has been deposited in the account you drew the check on, but it will leave you with ten dollars."

"What am I supposed to do?" Brian asked with shock.

"Get a job," Lydia said. "For the next month, you need to work to support yourself." She nodded to Emily.

"Work is good for the soul," his grandfather continued. "It makes a man a man. I worked my entire life to earn the money my children and grandchildren are intent on spending. So for the next month you will be allowed two hundred and fifty dollars a week for food and lodging, and it won't go far. You also need to get a job. At the end of the month, you must bring the money you've earned, or what's left of it, to Mrs. Maxwell. She will decide if you have the mettle to pass the test."

Brian expected the video to end, but it didn't.

"You can walk away and tell me to go to hell, which I suspect in one way or another you've done already. But Brian, I have faith in you. If I didn't, I would never have gone to this trouble."

The video screen was paused again, and Lydia passed over a plain white envelope. Brian opened it and found cash.

"That is all I can give you until next week. The first order of business is going to be for you to find a place to live. I suggest you contact some of your friends to see if they'll let you stay with them."

Brian already had a pretty good idea that wasn't an option.

"Then you'll need to get a job. Do you have any marketable skills?" She tilted her eyebrows, telling him she already thought she knew the answer.

"Is that all?" Brian asked, more than a little overwhelmed.

"No. You cannot ask your father or family for help. If you do, it's over."

"What does 'it's over' mean? Do I get my trust fund, car, and condo back?"

She smiled and indicated to Emily once again. Dammit, had his grandfather thought of everything?

"Brian, I know what I'm asking of you isn't easy, but there are things you need to learn, and I'm hoping that once you do, you will become the man I wished I'd taken the time in person to see to it that you'd become. I see so much of your mother in you, and at times it hurts how similar to her you are."

His grandfather paused and looked toward something off screen before turning back, wiping his eyes. Brian had never seen his grandfather show this type of emotion before.

"If you decide to go through with this, I promise you'll learn not only a great deal about yourself, but a lot about the people around you as well. Lydia will be available if you truly get into trouble. Spend the month learning to rely on yourself."

The screen went blank, and Brian stood up to leave. He had no idea where he could find a place to live and how to go about getting a job.

Brian left the office, stepping outside into the brilliant spring sunshine. He wasn't sure where to go or how to start. There were missions and flophouses, but he had no intention of going there. In the end, he started walking back the way he'd come on the bus. There was nowhere he had to be at the moment, and maybe a walk would clear his head and help him figure out what the hell he was going to do.

BRIAN ENDED up walking and talking. Well, the talking part was more like pleading with people who didn't give a shit. Word about the restaurant had clearly gotten around to all his friends, and suddenly the people who a few days earlier could get together on a few hours' notice, all had other very important plans or sudden trips out of town or simply weren't taking his calls. The bastards. Once again he nearly slammed his phone onto the sidewalk. Instead he found a newspaper near a bench and picked it up before sitting down. He had to find a job, and he figured he might as well start with the Help Wanted ads.

After spending half an hour reading each one, he shoved the paper into the trash. Lydia had been right—he wasn't qualified for anything, and the few jobs he might be able to get turned his stomach. He was not going to wash dishes. The restaurants that were looking were all ones he and his friends frequented, and he was not going to allow the ungrateful losers to see his ultimate downfall.

He continued on, passing into a small business area to the north of the city. Prospect Place was a renewed neighborhood in the heart of the city, with a small shopping center and new condos. There were restaurants, and one place had a Help Wanted sign out front. He sighed and went in.

A health club. Brian wondered how he'd missed the sign out front. Hell, he'd been paying more attention to his own thoughts than where he was going, so he was probably lucky he hadn't been hit crossing a street. Hadn't Cade said he worked at a health club? Brian knew there weren't many downtown, so it came as no surprise when he saw his benefactor from last night standing behind the desk.

"Brian," Cade said. "I didn't know you were a member."

"I'm not." He wasn't sure where to begin.

"How did things go? Did everything get straightened out?" Cade stepped back and checked in a woman in pink workout gear before returning to him.

"Not exactly." Brian shook his head. "I have to get a job and find a place to live. It seems…. It's too complicated to explain, but it all has to do with my grandfather's will. It'll get straightened out eventually, but until then I'm rather stuck. I saw the sign out front and wondered what kind of job was available."

"I'll check," Cade said. He held up a finger before opening a door behind him. He disappeared for a little while, then returned. "It's a floater position. Basically you'd help out in a number of areas when it's needed. You'd work the desk, and they'll probably have you assist the trainers, stuff like that. The work here isn't hard, and they treat me pretty well. I can get you an application if you like."

Brian nodded. What choice did he have? He needed a job of some sort, and he needed it fast. Cade brought him the paper and a pen, and Brian began filling out the form. He supposed this was something people did all the time, but he had never seen anything like this before, and when they asked for experience, he tried to think of something to put in that section but ended up leaving it blank. He signed at the bottom and passed it back to Cade.

"I'll take it to the manager," he said with his usual energy.

Brian was coming to realize that was Cade's normal state, and as he watched him work and interact with the members, he found that energy catching. Cade smiled and was genuinely happy to see them as they came in, and almost everyone left with a smile.

"He says he'll talk to you," Cade told him and opened the half door in the reception counter so Brian could come around. At least this was promising.

He went into the cluttered office and sat in the only chair across from a desk with a large computer monitor and stacks of papers. Obviously this was also a kind of storage area, because there were cases of energy bars stacked in one corner.

"Brian, I'm Garrett, the manager of the club."

"It's good to meet you," Brian said, shaking the offered hand. This was a completely new situation for him, but Brian wrapped himself in confidence and hoped like hell it covered up his uncertainty.

"Why are you applying for a job with us?" Garrett asked.

"I need one and saw your sign out front," Brian said. He realized he needed to be a little vague, and the fact that he needed a job because his very rich grandfather had made it some sort of twisted condition in his will probably wasn't going to go over very well.

"When he was in here, Cade said you helped him in the park. He said he was mugged, and you caught the guy."

Garrett smiled, and Brian understood that might be his way in.

"Yeah, well, it was as much dumb luck as anything else. I put myself in the guy's way and used him as a cushion. He wasn't in the best of shape with me falling on him, and the police got there really fast." It was honest, and yet it didn't make him sound like a complete doofus, he hoped.

"Most people would have gotten out of the way and let the guy pass. What you did meant a lot to Cade." Garrett turned to look over the application. "I have to ask. You're twenty-five, and you've never had a job before? That seems a little strange. Are you trying to hide something?"

"No. I've never had a job outside of my family, and I need one now."

"Why is that?"

Brian shrugged. "I need to eat and find a place to live, and to do that I have to work." He knew he was being evasive, but his name was probably enough of a giveaway as it was. "My family has cut me out, and I need to make my own way." That was truthful. "I wish I could tell you I have a number of great skills, but I am smart, so I can learn to do just about anything."

"Let me call your references," Garrett said.

He'd given Lydia as a reference because he couldn't think of anyone else. Brian left the office and closed the door, making a call right away.

"Lydia Maxwell please," he said when the phone was answered. He was put through to her office, where Emily took the call.

"She's in a meeting."

"It's Brian Paulson," he said and was asked to hold.

"Yes, Brian," Lydia said in a businesslike manner.

"I have a line on a job, and they're going to call my references. I didn't know who else to name, so I asked them to contact you," Brian said, hearing the half-pleading tone in his voice. He hated it, but it was how he felt.

"Already?" She sounded surprised. "I have to give you credit for moving fast."

"It's at a health club for a floater position. I'm not sure what that is exactly, but a friend works there."

"One of your friends would work at a health club?" She sounded like she was going to start laughing. "They don't seem like the type."

"He's a new friend, I guess." Brian turned toward the door, watching Cade as he worked. The guy always seemed to be moving and smiling. "He helped me last night."

"Very well, I'll do what I can." She hung up, and Brian put his phone away. It wasn't very often that he was on pins and needles, especially over some job that the day before he wouldn't have thought twice about. In fact he couldn't figure out why he was going through all this after all. He could simply walk away, and that would be that. Whatever games his grandfather was playing would die with him, and Brian would go on with his life.

Brian sat on one of the benches as people continued to come and go, each of them with a smile from Cade or a wave good-bye. He hated wasting time, but sitting there watching Cade was a pleasure. He had huge blue eyes and a cute swoopy nose, with full red lips and cheeks that formed little dimples that seemed almost ever present. He never stopped moving and was dressed cleanly, but in no way fancy. Cade knew what he was doing, and his energy filled the room. No wonder the club had hired him for the front desk. He was perfect for it. He smiled at everyone as they came in and said good-bye to them when they left. What could possibly leave a better impression?

Garrett came out of his office and approached him, walking around the desk. "I have some paperwork you need to fill out and sign. We can start you tomorrow at opening. You need to be here at ten minutes before six."

Brian opened his mouth to ask if he meant six in the morning but snapped it shut. Instead he nodded and wondered how in the hell he was going to get up that early in the morning. Of course that brought up the bigger question of where he was going to be spending the night. He had a job; that was the first step. Now he needed a place to stay. What a pain in the rear end, especially when he had a perfectly wonderful and comfortable place just a few miles away.

"All right," he answered, already feeling tired at the thought.

Garrett handed him the forms, and Brian took a seat to fill them out.

"You don't have a place to go, do you?" Cade asked from just behind the counter.

"No. Things are more messed up than I thought." That was the simplest explanation. "My grandfather died, and in his will he set up all these things that I have to do. Part of that is having everything taken away from me. I suspect I'll get it back, but not until I do what he wants or learn whatever it is he thinks I need to." Brian continued filling out the forms. He had the rudimentary information he needed and managed to complete them, using his Cudahy Towers address. "I have a little money, but I know it's not enough for the entire month."

"You are welcome to my sofa if you want," Cade offered. "I work here until three, and I'm off at the restaurant, so you can come by here then."

"Thanks," Brian said. At least he knew where he was going to be tonight. After that he wasn't sure, but he'd take it a day at a time.

"I have to go to the grocery store after work."

Cade looked at him expectantly, and Brian nodded. He had been given money for food, so he could pay. Other patrons came in, and once Brian had finalized things with Garrett, he left the club, feeling pretty good about things until he realized he was hungry. He walked across the street to one of the many restaurants in the area. He actually sat down and looked at the menu and was about to order when he noticed the prices for the first time. They were something he never paid attention to, and now he practically gasped when he realized he was about to pay a hefty share of the cash in his pocket for a single meal. For the second time in as many days, he flushed with embarrassment in a restaurant and left, this time without leaving a bill behind. He'd asked when he was going to be paid and found out it would be two weeks, and he'd only be paid for his first week. So the money he had on him needed to last, and God knew what else was going to happen.

HE MET Cade at three, spending much of the day wandering around and wasting time. He had no place to be, and none of his usual pastimes were feasible, as they usually meant spending quite a bit of money at some of the city's nicer stores.

"Are you ready?" Brian asked when he saw Cade come out of the club. Brian had been sitting on a bench watching people pass, and he was more than a little bored of it.

"Sure. This way." Cade tilted his head and led the way down the sidewalk.

"We're going shopping, right?" Brian had been to a grocery store only a few times in his life. He had Maria to do things like that for him.

"Yes."

"Can I ask how you get the groceries home when you're done?" Brian had expected some sort of conveyance to appear.

Cade laughed. "I carry them. I always have to make sure they're packed properly, and if I have a lot, I take the bus, but that has its own problems too. Today, since you're with me, I can get more than I normally would, and we'll ride the bus home, which stops at the corner near the store."

"But what about things like milk and juice that are heavy?" Brian asked.

"I don't buy them unless I can carry them, and since I need a lot of things right now, I'll do without the milk. And for juice, I buy the frozen kind in cans. It's lighter. Since it's warm, we have to be careful of frozen things, even on the bus, so ice cream is totally out."

Cade trudged on as though what he'd said was perfectly acceptable and normal. Brian had never done without anything. He always had a refrigerator and cupboards full of whatever he wanted without thought. If he didn't have it, Maria got it.

"Sounds like a lot of planning," Brian commented as they turned the corner and walked into the grocery store parking lot.

Cade shrugged and led the way inside, taking a cart and starting down the first aisle. Brian watched what Cade bought: plenty of fresh vegetables, very few cans, pasta, and the frozen juice like he'd mentioned. Some meat. There were no snacks or junk food, no processed anything. By the time they checked out, the contents of the cart were very basic and Brian noticed, rather inexpensive, at least by comparison to the other items in the store.

When it came time to check out, Brian waited until the total was announced and gave Cade half of it. He expected that Cade didn't normally buy this much food and was expanding his purchases because of him. Cade double bagged all the groceries and parceled them out for carrying. Brian felt like a pack mule but said nothing, even though a grumble rumbled in his throat.

They ended up waiting for the bus. Brian went to set down his bags, but Cade stopped him.

"The concrete will scratch and weaken them, and then at some point they'll split open, and we'll be stuck."

Brian rolled his eyes and stood, waiting in the shade of the store, hoping like hell that no one he knew drove by. Finally the bus pulled up, and they filed on with everyone else. Somehow Brian managed to get the pass that Lydia had given him out of his pocket while everyone behind him became impatient. It was on the tip of his tongue to snap at them, but fuck it all, he was the stranger in their world. It was his fault for not being ready.

"It's okay," Cade said once they sat down and the bus pulled away. "Most people know the routine, and they're just anxious to get home."

Brian nodded, bags resting on his lap, watching as the bus pulled away and into traffic.

"Could this thing go any slower?" Brian asked himself ten minutes later. They stopped at every street corner, it seemed like, and his legs were going to sleep. By the time Cade indicated they were getting off, Brian figured they could have walked and gotten there faster. Still, he was glad he'd kept quiet three blocks later when his arms were aching to beat all hell.

"Thank God," Brian moaned when he set the groceries on Cade's small table. Cade, on the other hand, went right to work putting everything away.

"There are glasses in the cupboard and ice in the freezer. Just be sure to fill a tray when you empty it."

He continued working while he pattered on, saying strange things that Brian had no clue about. He got a glass and went to the refrigerator, wondering where the ice and water dispensers were. He filled the glass from the sink and finally opened the freezer looking for the ice. He eventually found it but managed to spill water all over the floor when he had to refill the tray things.

"What do you do in the evenings?" Brian asked as he went into the living room to sit down on the couch.

39

"Well, after I make dinner, I have to do laundry, because I don't get many evenings off like this, and I have to make the most of them. That'll pretty much be the whole evening, because I have to sit in the laundry room or someone might take my clothes." Cade sat down next to him. "That's all you have to wear, isn't it?"

Cade looked him over, and Brian realized he was still in the same clothes from the night before. He should have gotten some things he needed at the store, but he hadn't thought of it.

"Yeah," Brian said. He wondered how he was going to get more on the small amount of money he had.

Cade finished his water and stood. "Drink up. We need to get you some things."

Brian drank his water like he'd been in the desert and put the glass in the sink.

APPARENTLY A trip to get clothes meant another ride on the bus to some sort of clothing store Brian had not only never seen but that left him cold. "What is this?"

"The Goodwill Store. You can get really decent clothes for only a few dollars."

Brian followed Cade off the bus and into the store, more than a little wary of what he was going to find. Cade led him straight to the racks and began looking at things. It took Brian only a minute to realize that these weren't new clothes. He shuddered at the thought of wearing what someone else had worn. That went against everything…. He was known for his style, and now he had to get clothes other people had worn.

"This is great," Cade said, handing him a shirt that didn't look hideous, but Brian only dared touch the hanger, and even then he just let it drape over his finger. "What's wrong?" Cade asked, turning his puppy-dog eyes in Brian's direction before leaning closer. "This too much for you?" The happy look was gone. "Real people can't always afford silk shirts." He fingered the fabric of the one he had on. "Or designer pants. Sometimes times are hard, and we shop at secondhand stores." Cade pulled out another pair of pants. "These have been washed, but we'll do it again when we get them home. They'll be clean, and you won't have to wear the same thing for a third day." Cade turned up his nose. "They're getting a little ripe."

"Gee, thanks, I wasn't expecting to get shut out of my home," Brian retorted.

"Look around. Half the people in here have probably been evicted or turned out of somewhere at one point in their lives. We work hard but don't always have piles of money." Cade turned back to the rack and pulled out another couple of shirts. Then he snatched them all from Brian. "You'd better start looking if you don't want to be here all day."

Cade turned away, and Brian realized those shirts hadn't been for him. Brian started looking and found a few things. The thought of actually wearing them was uncomfortable to say the least, but he needed fresh clothes badly. So he found some things that were acceptable and then turned to pants. He figured jeans would work and got two pairs in his size. He needed underwear but drew the line at used. That was gross. They did have inexpensive things in packages, and he bought some, along with socks. When he brought it all to the counter, the woman rang him up and asked for less than twenty dollars. Brian paid and tried to think of the last time he'd bought anything for twenty dollars. The socks he was wearing probably cost more than that. Cade paid for his purchases as well, and then they trooped back out and got on the bus once more.

Brian sat with his purchases on his lap, staring out the window, thinking of nothing. It was the best he could do not to dwell on the fact that he had just bought someone else's clothes.

The entire ride, he and Cade didn't talk. They got off the bus early, and Cade led him into a drugstore.

"You need stuff," Cade said.

Brian browsed, but nothing was familiar. He ended up getting a toothbrush, razors, shaving cream, toothpaste, and some deodorant. Of course none of them were the organic, natural-scented things he had at home that Maria always made sure never ran out. The bill was more than the clothes, and they left the store with Brian figuring how much money he had left for the week. What he'd been given had certainly gone down fast.

In the apartment, Cade gave him a little space to put the things he'd gotten and then let him use the bathroom. "I'm going to put this stuff in the laundry," Cade said as he handed Brian a set of clothes. "Clean up, and come down to the basement when you're done." Cade retrieved a clothes basket and added the clothes Brian had just bought to the pile, with the exception of the socks and underwear that Brian was going to need.

"Okay," Brian said.

"Be sure to lock the door behind you. I have my key." Cade left the apartment, and Brian used the bathroom. It felt good to be clean, shaved, and have his teeth brushed. He dressed in the clothes Cade had given him, amazed that they fit. The sweatpants must have been a little big on Cade. They were soft, and when he inhaled, they smelled a little like Cade. He found he liked that, and he sniffed his shirt more than once before putting on his shoes and leaving the apartment, locking the door as Cade instructed.

The basement was pretty dreary, it was unpainted, and a few machines were against the wall. Cade sat at a table reading by the light of a few fluorescent tubes. Brian bit back a comment and sat down across from him.

"So what do we do now?"

"The washers will be done in half an hour, and then we move everything to the dryers. That takes an hour, and then we fold everything." Cade looked up from what he was reading. "I'll stay here until the stuff goes in the dryers and then go make some dinner while you watch them from there."

The idea sounded about as interesting as watching paint dry or sitting on the edge of a golf course seeing how fast grass grew. He refrained from rolling his eyes. "Is that what you really do?"

"I can't afford to buy new clothes, so yeah…."

The derision in his voice raised Brian's hackles.

"This forced impoverishment may be some kind of game to you and your family, but this is my life. I have to make my own way and look out for myself without a trust fund safety net."

Damn, that stung more than it should have. "I make my own way." His words sounded feeble to his own ears.

"Yeah, right. Let me guess, today you got your very first job ever. I bet you can't remember the last time you were up at five in the morning."

Brian gulped. He'd forgotten he was going to have to be up at the ass crack of dawn. And what was worse was that he couldn't deny what Cade had said.

"All your life you went to fancy schools and had everything you could possibly want handed to you. I had none of that. My mom raised me and my brother alone. There was no father, and the only money we had was what she earned from working two jobs. I took care of my brother after I got home from school."

"You have a younger brother, then," Brian observed.

"No. My brother is eighteen months older. He has learning challenges, so when I was old enough, I helped take care of him. By the time I was in second grade I could cook basic things, do laundry and dishes, clean the house, and put Phillip to bed. I had to read him a story or he'd never go to sleep, so I learned to read faster than the other kids." Cade set the magazine he was reading on the table with a slight smack of the paper.

"I didn't have it exactly easy. My father will never win parent of the year. My mom was pretty cool, though… when she was around, which wasn't all that often."

Cade rolled his eyes. "I bet there was always food on the table and you had a big house to live in. Our apartment for three people was smaller than this. The three of us had one bedroom, and Mom slept in the living room. So whatever you're thinking about how sorry you feel for yourself, just stop it. You aren't going to get any sympathy from me." Cade stood and strode out of the laundry room. "I'll be back in a few minutes."

Brian stared after Cade and swore under his breath. "Fucking hell," he muttered. He thought about going after him but stayed where he was. What in the heck was he going to say to Cade once he caught him? Brian was so lost most of the time. Truth be told, he'd probably been lost for a long time, but he covered it with parties, drinking, and plenty of sex.

He watched the door, but Cade didn't return. The machines stopped, and Brian went over, wondering what he should do. Finally Cade strode back in and nudged him out of the way. Brian stepped back and let Cade move the clothes. He put coins in the machines and then turned and was about to leave again.

"Cade," Brian said, wondering what else could make this better. "I'm sorry" was on the tip of his tongue, but that was most likely the wrong thing to say. "Thank you."

That stopped him in his tracks. "What the hell for?"

"Everything," Brian said. "I know you're mad, and I'm trying to figure out why, but you were nice enough to try to help me."

Cade walked back to the chair he'd been sitting in a while earlier. "You've had it lucky for a long time, and you don't even know it." Cade sat down. One of the machines stopped, and Cade jumped up and banged it on the side until it began running again.

"I suppose luck is all in the beholder. Yeah, I had money, but that was about all."

Cade shook his head. "Maybe we always want what we don't have, but a little bit of your money would have gone a long way to helping my mom. We didn't even need much, but she worked all the time to try to keep us fed and clothed." Cade picked up the magazine again. "How many times did you go hungry?"

Brian blinked. "Me…?"

"See. Try getting through when your last meal was lunch at school and the next one was going to be breakfast just before school." Cade's gaze was knife hard. "Sometimes there wasn't enough, so I made sure Phillip got something to eat, and maybe that meant I ate a few crackers for dinner because that was all there was in the house."

"Dang," Brian groaned. "I never had that. My mom died when I was twelve. She was a doctor and was working in a clinic in Africa. She contracted one of the diseases she was trying to fight and lost the battle. After that my dad met someone else, so I was shipped off to boarding school and pretty much forgotten. Dad had a new bimbo wife, and my aunt and uncle were too wrapped up in their own families and self-centered lives. My grandmother tried to help, but she died less than a year later. So then I was left with my grandfather, who…. Well, why should I have expected any of them to give a fuck, so I guess I didn't."

"Well, crap. At least I had a family who cared."

"See, there's a shitty side to everything."

"Is that Brian's wisdom of life?" Cade asked. "Because it sounds depressing."

"You were just complaining about your own life, so…."

Cade nodded slowly. "We may have had it hard, but we had each other. My brother did the simple things he could. Phillip used to like dusting, so the house was always clean. He dusted every day when he got home from school. He also took the trash out to the cans. Repetitive things that don't change work well for him, and he likes doing them. At school I used to get presents sometimes at Christmas. A coloring book and crayons were like gold to him. He'd spend hours coloring, so I gave him what I got." Cade shrugged.

"You gave your brother your Christmas present?" That was unfathomable to Brian.

"It made him happy," Cade answered, as though it were the most logical answer in the world. "I need to make some dinner. So

45

once the machines are done, put the clothes in the basket and bring them back up to the apartment."

Brian agreed, and Cade left the laundry room.

WHEN BRIAN returned to the apartment, Cade was putting sandwiches on the table. Brian wondered if that was all there was, but he said nothing. He'd already put his foot in it enough, so he decided that since Cade was willing to share his apartment and dinner with him, he should be grateful about it. He figured his grandmother would be pleased.

"I know it isn't what you're used to." Cade put two glasses of ice water on the table and then added small bowls of salad for each of them, and a bottle of dressing clunked in the center of the table.

Brian put the basket on the sofa, and Cade rushed over to pull out shirts and pants, then hurried to the bedroom. When he returned, he handed Brian his clothes on two hangers.

"If you don't hang the shirts up right away, they wrinkle, and I hate ironing."

Brian hung them where Cade had shown him earlier, and then they sat down to eat. The small salad and sandwich didn't abate Brian's hunger completely, and he wondered if there was more to eat that Cade hadn't brought out, but once the dishes were cleared away, he got the idea that was it, until Cade brought out a container of cookies, parceling out two each.

"My mom made these." He acted like they were gold. "She never gets much time, and they're my favorite, so I try to make them last."

"My grandmother used to make something like these," Brian said as he took a bite. They were basic chocolate chip cookies but tasted special. He wondered why and came to the conclusion that it had to be because they were special to Cade.

"Are you up to doing dishes?"

Cade cleared the table. Brian figured dishes were the least he could do. He had washed dishes and done basic chores while he was at boarding school. He located the soap and filled the sink with water. Cade left him alone. Thank goodness. Brian managed to get soap all over himself, and while the dishes came out clean, he'd made a mess doing it and had to clean that up as well.

It took twice as long as it should have to wash a few dishes, but once they were drying in the rack, he let the water out and washed down the suds and his arms and hands. "Do you need me to put them away?"

"No. They can dry there."

Cade turned on the television and flipped channels. Brian joined him and watched as the six or seven channels repeated themselves.

"I just get the basic stations."

Brian nodded and kept his mouth shut. At home he had every station known to exist, and he never gave it a single thought. They settled on watching a rerun, and after a while Cade got a phone call that he took in the other room. Brian paid little attention and continued watching until Cade brought out the same stack of blankets Brian had used the night before.

"Night," Cade said. "We need to get up really early to make it into work on time. I wasn't supposed to go in that early, but Garrett wants me to train you for part of the day."

Cade was already yawning, and after he used the bathroom, Brian took his turn, changed and got under the covers, then watched down the tiny hallway toward Cade's room with its closed door.

Brian knew he needed to go to sleep, but he was wide awake, and his mind was determined to run at full steam, mulling over what his grandfather truly wanted of him and if Brian really cared enough to continue whatever was going on with this will. He lost track of however long he lay there and was finally going to sleep when he heard the snick of a door opening. There was just enough light for him to see Cade walk across the hall to the bathroom.

When he turned on the light, for a brief second, he caught a glimpse of Cade's bare chest. Cade wasn't really muscular, but he was trim and lithe. Brian clamped his eyes closed so Cade wouldn't see him watching and then waited until he finished, hoping for another glance when he went back to his room.

CHAPTER 4

BRIAN WAS dragging, and he and Cade were just arriving at the club. It had been barely light when they'd gotten up, dressed, and had eaten a little. His stomach did a little jig as they got off the bus and walked to the back entrance of the club. Cade rang the bell, and when the door was opened, they went inside.

"Is Garrett here already?"

"No," Sam said as he relocked the door.

"This is Brian. He's starting this morning. Sam is the assistant manager," Cade explained.

"Garrett left a list of things he wants Brian to do, and he said you were going to work with him this morning." Sam sounded stressed. "I have clients starting in half an hour, so I'm not going to have much time today."

"Sam is also a personal trainer," Cade said with a smile, and Brian noticed that Cade was trying not to look at Sam too often. Sam was well built, to say the least, and the T-shirt he wore was stretched to capacity by a full chest and bulging arms.

"I'll get him started and handle the desk." Cade took the list and looked it over with an amused expression. "Let's get going. The club opens soon." Cade hurried toward the stairs. The halls were dark, but soon lights came on. "This is the cleaning closet, and you'll need to start here."

"I'm not on the desk?" Brian asked. He had seen himself checking people in and out, talking to people, maybe selling memberships.

"No. You're a floater. So that means you do anything and everything that needs to be done. We need the showers in the men's locker room cleaned. So fill the mop bucket and scrub down the floor and the base of the walls. Guys will be coming in, so you'll want to get that done as quickly as possible."

Cade began filling the bright yellow roller bucket, and Brian stayed out of the way, shocked that he was expected to clean.

"I'm really a janitor?" he asked derisively.

"This is your job. Garrett asked you to do it, so you do it, if you want to stay employed." He turned off the water and placed the hose back in the large sink. Then he put the mop in the bucket and pushed it toward Brian. "I'll show you where to go, and then I need to get upstairs."

He hurried down the hall, and Brian morosely followed with the bucket.

The locker room smelled of sweat and men. Hell, the tiles had probably soaked up the scent after years of use. Cade held open the glass door to the large single-room shower area.

"Just wash the floors and lower walls and turn on the showers to rinse them. Be careful or you'll end up soaked, and you don't want to be wet the rest of the day."

Cade left, and Brian groaned as he slopped the mop around the floor in no particular pattern or order.

It took him a few minutes to realize that he should have started in the far corner. The floor was slippery, but he managed to get everything mopped and pushed the bucket out of the area before catching his foot on the edge of one of the rubber mats. He nearly went down and ended up slopping the mop water everywhere. He swore and thanked goodness that there were drains all along the floor. Not wanting to press his luck, he turned on one of the showers and sprayed down as much of the floor as he could before making a hasty retreat back into the locker room.

Grant Marcus, a friend of a friend, sat on the edge of the nearest bench. Brian had honestly never expected he'd see anyone he knew there, but it figured. He rolled the mop bucket through and swore Grant half looked at him, but he continued getting changed. Brian was out the door before Grant could give him another look. Then he hurried down to the mop closet and up the stairs to where Cade stood behind the desk. "What else do I do?" he asked, hoping it was something where he could stay out of sight.

"Just beyond the showers is the pool area. You need to hose down the steam room sometime this morning, when it's empty, and clean the sauna floor. When you're done, let me know, and I'll show you how to check the whirlpool chemicals."

THE REST of the morning went much the same. Cade showed him what to do, and Brian tried not to mess it up or make a bigger mess while hiding the fact that he had no idea what he was doing. Every task was strange and seemed manually stupid.

"Brian," Sam called as he was about ready to go to lunch. "Did you check the chemicals in the whirlpool?"

"Yes, I did it with him. It was a little off, and we equalized it out," Cade answered. "He also checked the pool, and it was good. Why?"

"Someone made a mess in it a few minutes ago," Sam said.

Cade groaned.

"I closed it, but we're going to need to drain, clean, and refill it."

"Okay. I'll do that," Cade volunteered. He turned to Brian. "Go get something to eat. There's a diner a block away that has sandwiches and stuff. When you get back, come find me in the pool area. This is going to take a while."

The thought of what might have happened in the whirlpool had him skipping out of the club as fast as he could, and he nearly knocked Peter over as he was hurrying in.

"Hey," Peter said with surprise and more than a touch of wariness. "What are you doing here?" Peter's grin slid off his face when his gaze drifted to Brian's chest and his name badge. "You work here?"

Brian swallowed hard. "Yeah."

"What are you doing?" Peter looked him over. "Working the desk? It isn't personal training."

Peter's mouth hung open, and Brian stepped aside without answering.

"Oh my God, you're the pool-cleaning guy, aren't you?" Peter dropped his bag and nearly doubled over with laughter. "What would your family say if they knew?"

"Jesus," Brian swore, his anger rising. "What did I ever do to you? I was your friend, and you act like an asshole."

"Hey, I was just teasing. So this whole restaurant thing wasn't just a blip. What's going on? Did your grandfather cut you off in his will?"

"Something like that," Brian said and checked his watch. "If you're through being a jerk, I have to grab lunch and get back to work." He had no fucking idea on earth why he was taking this shit job so seriously. Maybe it was because he didn't want Cade to look bad.

"Yeah. You wouldn't want to be late to scrub the toilets," Peter said, continuing to laugh as he went inside. Brian wanted to follow him and rip the fucker's head off. What a piece of crap. Instead he hurried to the diner Cade had told him about and in a flash of goodwill got two sandwiches and sodas to go and carried them back to the club, where he didn't run into Peter again... at least not right away.

Cade was in the pool area when he joined him. "I got us sandwiches," he told Cade, who was in gloves, scrubbing the walls of the whirlpool.

"I'm almost done, and then we can fill it. The water will be cold, so it'll have to be closed for the rest of the day until it warms up and the chemical balance is right." Cade climbed out and pulled off the heavy gloves. "This is the whirlpool access. I have everything shut off. I need to close the drain"—he demonstrated—"and then turn on the water to fill it."

Cade reached back into the room, and Brian grabbed his waist so he didn't overbalance. Cade turned the water on and straightened up.

When he turned, Brian got a close look into Cade's amazing, lively eyes, and he froze. Other guys had caught his attention, but with Cade there was something special. He blinked as it hit him that he actually cared what Cade thought of him. Peter was a pain in the ass and an overgrown frat boy. But Cade was different. He couldn't put his finger on exactly why, though. On the outside Cade was always happy, but there was sadness and weight in his eyes that Brian didn't know the source of.

"We should eat before your lunch period is over," Cade whispered.

"Don't we need to watch this?" Brian asked.

"No. It takes an hour to fill, so we have time."

Cade swallowed, and Brian found the way his throat worked fascinating. Brian turned away, and they went out of the area and down the hallway to the small employee break area. Brian had put their lunches on the table, and after washing their hands, they sat down to eat.

Brian had about ten minutes left, so he ate quickly while Cade told him what else he needed to do. "Tomorrow I'll train you on the front desk, and then you'll know almost all there is. The job here isn't complicated, but there's a lot of parts to it, especially when Jason, the guy who does most of the cleaning, is out for vacation. It'll settle down when he gets back next week."

When he was done eating, Brian threw away the trash and left the break room, nearly bumping into Peter as he walked toward the weight room. This time Peter said nothing and actually seemed to pretend he hadn't seen him. Brian wasn't sure what was more aggravating. He wanted to beat the crap out of his one-time friend, but he went on to work instead.

By the end of his first day, Brian's arms ached from mopping everything. He and Cade left a little after two and went right back to the apartment. Brian lay on the sofa, exhausted from having gotten up so early. His muscles ached in places he hadn't known could hurt. Thank God he was done for the day.

Cade came out of the bedroom and went right into the bath. Water ran, and when Cade returned, he was clean and dressed.

"I'll see you later tonight. There's some sandwich fixings for dinner and a bowl of potato salad."

Cade left the apartment, and Brian wondered how Cade could go from job to job like that without being completely worn out.

Brian didn't do much that afternoon but rest and wonder how Cade was doing. It was nearly eleven by the time Cade came home from the restaurant, dragging and tired. Brian had never thought about how hard some people worked to survive. Brian had already made up his bed and was under the covers.

Cade sat in the chair, and Brian got up for some water.

"Are you hungry?"

"No. I ate at work. I really just need to go to bed," Cade murmured. "I checked the schedule, and you need to be at the club at six and me at eight."

Cade said good night and went to his room. Brian turned out the lights and went right to sleep.

BRIAN CAME home from the club two days later to find Cade frantically moving around the apartment. The kitchen table had been transformed into an art station, with papers, colored pencils, coloring books, and crayons. It was Cade's day off, from both jobs apparently.

"What's going on?"

"My mother called. She got called into work, and the care provider is off, so she asked if Phillip could spend the evening here."

Cade continued bustling. The bedding that Brian had left in a pile on the sofa had been put away, and everything was vacuumed and cleaned to within an inch of its life.

"Do you need help?"

Cade paused in midstride. "You're welcome to stay if you like, but I'll understand if you'd rather be somewhere else."

"I can go if you want me to," Brian said. After all, he'd been staying as Cade's guest, and he didn't have any rights here. Brian would figure something out if he had to.

"It isn't that." Cade put down the dust cloth and walked around the sofa. "Phillip is a little smaller than me and… he's…. Phillip is perpetually about six or seven years old. There are some things he does very well, but with most things he's like a child. Phillip loves to color and do puzzles, and he's as kind and caring as anyone you'll ever meet." The nervousness Brian had seen when they first met had returned in spades. "I love him very much, but he can be…. Phillip doesn't understand boundaries very well. He might hug you or completely ignore you. It's hard to tell, and he can be hard to understand."

"All right."

"Phillip is also strong, and he doesn't always understand what to do with it." Cade blinked a few times. "Phillip isn't like the perfect people you're friends with. He's his own person and has his own personality, but he spills when he eats and sometimes says things that…."

"If you want me to leave, I certainly can. I'll understand if you want some time alone with him. I have been around a lot." Brian swallowed. "Maybe too much. I know this is… unusual, and I appreciate you helping me."

"I like having you here. It's nice, and I'm much less lonely." Cade seemed to snap out of what had come over him for a second. "Phillip loves meeting new people, and he'll probably talk your ear off. But… some of my other friends met him, and he made them uncomfortable, so I thought I'd give you an out if you wanted to take it."

A knock on the door seemed to settle everything, because the door opened and a man a little smaller than Cade, but who looked like him, ran inside, throwing himself at Cade with everything he had.

"Hi, Phillip," Cade said with a grin.

"I missed you so much."

Phillip demonstrated by squeezing Cade tighter, and Brian chuckled at Cade's slightly bulged eyes. He understood what Cade was saying about Phillip's enthusiasm.

"What did I say about going easy on people?" a woman asked from the doorway, and Phillip backed away. She had the same eyes as Cade and the same bright smile.

"It's okay, Mom," Cade said, hugging his brother back. "I set up the table with things for you, and there are videos you can watch if you want." Cade was already getting his brother settled. "This is my friend Brian. He's been staying here for a few days."

Phillip came over and shook his hand, giving him a huge crooked-tooth grin. "I'm Phillip," he said, his speech a little slurred but understandable.

"Brian, and it's a pleasure to meet you."

"Wanna color with me?" Phillip asked as he sat down at the table.

"I will in a few minutes," Brian said.

"I'm Shirley," the woman said, then turned to Cade. "I didn't know you had a friend staying with you. Is this *friendship* serious?"

"Mom. Brian is the man who helped me in the park, and he needed some help of his own. He's not going to be here for very long. There's just stuff going on in his life that he needs to deal with."

Cade skirted the story, and for that Brian was grateful.

"It's nice to meet you, and I appreciate what you did for Cade." Her smile was back. "I need to get to work, but I'll be back about ten." She hugged Cade and then left.

Brian sat at the table next to Phillip, who passed him a coloring book and pointed to the flower picture he wanted Brian to do. Brian took the colored pencils and got to work, sharing glances with Cade.

"Are you hungry?" Cade asked a while later.

He placed a plate of cookies on the table. Phillip barely looked up as he took one, putting it between his lips and continuing with his task.

"That's very good," Cade whispered to his brother and then came to look at Brian's picture. "Look at this, Phillip." Cade turned the coloring book so Phillip could see.

"So pretty. Are you an artist?" Phillip said with wide-eyed awe.

"No." Brian smiled and lifted his gaze to Cade. He was so close to him that Brian inhaled his sweet scent with woodsy undertones. "I used to like to draw when I was in school, but those particular skills weren't valued by the rest of my family. They were all about making money… or spending it." Brian turned the book and carefully removed the page. He signed it and handed the picture to Phillip.

"Make one for me," Cade said and rested his hand on Brian's shoulder.

Brian felt the heat from his hand through his shirt. Without thinking, he placed his hand on Cade's. It felt right, too right, and after a few seconds, he pulled it away and picked up his colored pencils.

When Phillip was done with his picture, he ate his cookie and then started coloring another page. Brian stopped what he was doing to watch him. Phillip was very methodical, making small strokes, his tongue between his teeth.

"Cade says that babies color outside the lines," Phillip explained when he saw Brian watching him. "I'm not a baby."

He went back to work, and Brian did the same.

"Are we having macaroni and cheese?"

The change of subject was almost comical, and Brian smiled.

"Yes. I know it's your favorite." Cade showed Brian the blue box on the counter.

"I haven't had that since…." Brian tried to remember. "My grandmother made it for me. She said it was terrible but that she loved me enough to make me awful food if I wanted it."

Brian chuckled at the memory and the fact that his grandmother had all the money in the world, but she still cooked and took care of him herself after his mother died. She'd made the mac and cheese and had added all kind of things to it until it was the best in the world.

"She sounds like something else."

"She was. Grandmother worked hard all her life, and I can't remember her ever saying an unkind word to anyone. Not that she didn't rule the family with an iron fist, to use my mom's term, but she was one of those people who you wanted to make happy. I know I did." Brian set down the pencil he'd been holding.

"We never knew our grandparents. Mom said our dad left after I was born, and Mom's family didn't approve of her 'living in sin,' so by extension they didn't approve of us." Cade walked over to the stove and began filling pots with water.

"Sometimes families suck," Brian said.

"You said a naughty word," Phillip scolded. "You need to put a quarter in the jar."

Phillip pointed to a glass jar on the counter, and Brian dug in his pockets and managed to find a quarter, which he dropped through the slot.

"Now say sorry."

Brian glanced at Cade, who shrugged.

"Sorry."

Phillip seemed satisfied and went back to coloring. Brian watched the brothers go about their work, both equally intent on their tasks. In a way, they were so much alike it was scary.

"Mom says I need to go to a home," Phillip informed them after working for a while.

"We talked about this. It's a good home with other people like you," Cade told Phillip. "You'll learn to cook and clean. You like to clean. They'll also teach you how to shop and help you take care of yourself. Mom and I will visit you, and you can come see us."

"I thought about it, and I don't want to go," Phillip declared stubbornly, folding his arms over his chest.

"Why?" Cade asked patiently. "You'll have a lot of friends, and you'll get a room of your own. It'll be bigger than the one you have now, and you can take your books. You'll even get a desk that you can color at whenever you want."

Phillip didn't answer.

"The home sounds really cool," Brian said. "I'd like a room of my own."

"They won't make me cookies the way Momma does," Phillip finally said.

Cade chuckled. "You know that no one makes cookies like Mom. She'll still make cookies for you, and you can go see her when you want. They'll also give you bus rides to baseball games and take you to the beach and the pool."

Brian was wondering what kind of place this really was. He caught Cade's eye.

"Phillip needs to be more self-sufficient, and the group home will help him learn some of the skills he'll need to survive on his own. He'll never be able to do it without help, but Mom is worried that if he doesn't start moving toward some sort of self-sufficiency, he never will."

"Where is the home?" Brian asked.

"Outside Mequon. It's run by a charity foundation, and they built it and have buses and even a pool. It's really nice. Each resident gets their own room." Cade tilted his head toward the hallway, and Brian got up and followed him. "We've been trying to save enough money to get him in for a year. We're almost there."

"Is that why you work two jobs?" Brian asked.

Cade nodded. "I've been trying to help Mom get him in. They're run by a nonprofit, but it isn't free. It's the best place of its kind in the area, and that's what we want for him. I know he'll be happy there, and Mom will have an easier time of it. She's been taking care of him for a long time, and Phillip is growing and showing more independence. We need to encourage it. But the process is hard getting him convinced, and it will be difficult paying for him. Mom and I will do it, though, because Phillip deserves a happy life."

Brian had no doubt Cade meant it.

"I'm beginning to realize that we all deserve a happy life." He wasn't sure how to go about building one for himself or if he'd done anything, ever, to have a reason to expect one. Cade definitely deserved a chance at a good life, though. Already Brian could see Cade spent much of his money and time working to help others rather than himself.

"Come back and color with me," Phillip called.

"My public awaits," Brian quipped, and Cade rolled his eyes.

They went back to their respective tasks, and Phillip put everything away and neatened up when Cade reminded him that dinner was almost ready. Phillip got out the placemats and with some coaching set the table before taking his place. Brian helped Cade as best he could with his butterfingers kitchen hands and ended up being told to just sit down.

"I guess I'm more a hindrance than a help," he told Phillip, who looked at him blankly before turning expectantly to Cade.

"He said that he was being a pain and needed to get out of the kitchen before he was a danger," Cade explained, and Phillip nodded once before licking his lips as Cade brought the first bowl to the table.

They ate dinner with Phillip telling stories about what was happening at home. They were rambling and at times hard for Bryan to follow, but Cade seemed to listen attentively and asked appropriate questions. The bond between them was obviously deep. Cade didn't try to translate what Phillip was saying, and that was fine. Brian didn't want to interrupt them. After dinner, he did the dishes and joined Cade and Phillip in front of the television, where they watched *Toy Story* and *Finding Nemo*, apparently two of Phillip's favorite movies.

"He's something else," Brian said when Cade shut the door after his mother left with Phillip, a little after ten. Brian had received an enthusiastic hug from Phillip before he left, and he wondered if his ribs were still intact.

"Phillip is one of the few truly kind souls I think I've ever met. There's no guile or deceit in him. If he does something wrong and you ask him about it, he says he did it and then waits for his punishment. Usually you feel bad enough that he gets away with it. But he's so innocent that you don't want to burst that bubble. He's happy and carefree, and I really want him to stay that way."

Brian nodded. He could see that. "Is there a reason why your mother is looking into having him go to a group home now?"

The hurt in Cade's eyes told him there was a definite reason and that it wasn't a happy one.

"Mom has been battling cancer for the last two years. She was diagnosed with breast cancer, and her treatment has been successful, but she's afraid it will come back. Mom has worked so long that I think she's wearing out. She raised both of us on her own, and the doctor says she's tired and needs a break. So Phillip needs to rely on her a little less, and she deserves her chance to be happy, and to do that I think we need to give her some room to breathe." He turned away toward the bathroom.

"You're a good son and brother," Brian said, realizing he'd never been either.

Cade went inside and closed the door without saying anything. Brian wasn't sure if he'd said something wrong, but Cade was suddenly subdued and quiet, which wasn't like him at all.

Brian waited for him to come out. When he did, he was carrying his clothes and dressed in a light pair of pajamas with Superman on them. They were appropriate, as far as he was concerned. Brian came closer to him. Cade stopped, eyes widening slightly.

"What are you doing?"

Brian didn't answer. He simply leaned closer, touching his lips to Cade's. "I've wanted to do that since that night in my condo when you stood looking out over the water."

"I don't understand. I'm just this poor kid scraping by, and yeah, you don't have any money now, but that will change, and so will your feelings for me." Cade put his hands on Brian's shoulders to hold him still. "You know that. Things will change, and it's inevitable that you'll go back to the life you had. So it's probably best if we keep things...."

Brian didn't let him finish. He circled his arms around Cade's, pushing them away and taking him by his shoulders. He tugged Cade closer, feeling for resistance but receiving none. When he tilted his head and took Cade's mouth with his lips, he pressed hard, tasting. He feasted on succulent, sweet lips that sent a charge of frantic energy racing through him. Cade felt right, and Brian pulled him closer, holding him in his arms, sharing his heat.

Cade was like a live wire, all energy and heat. Brian liked that. Both had been missing in his life for a long time. When he broke the kiss, allowing them to breathe, Cade stepped back in bemused, wide-eyed wonder for a few seconds, and Brian wondered how he'd react. He hoped Cade would come back into his arms and that Brian could carry him off into the bedroom for some intimate explorations. Cade blinked a few times, and Brian could almost hear the wheels of decision turning in Cade's head. When he licked his lips, Brian's excitement grew, tightening his pants and making his left foot tingle.

"Good night," Cade breathed and turned away, hurried to his bedroom and closed the door.

All Brian could do was watch after him in wonder. After a few minutes of hoping Cade would return, Brian took his turn in the bathroom and then returned to the living room, where he put out the lights and climbed under the covers. At home he had the most amazing bed, and this sofa wasn't the most comfortable place to sleep night after night, but being near Cade made the sofa a place fit for a king.

BRIAN DIDN'T sleep well for days. Every time he closed his eyes, he saw Cade, bare-chested, gasping for breath the way he had after they'd kissed. He wanted more from him, but he wasn't going to ask. Not yet. Everything had been so simple before all this happened with his grandfather. Brian had lived an easy life with few cares and only the pursuit of fun as a goal. He didn't worry about others or their feelings, and if he was horny, he found someone to slake his lust and to make him happy for a while. Then he went on. Brian lay on Cade's sofa, barely able to sleep for the third day in a row because his mind wouldn't turn off for a second. He wasn't sure what to do to get Cade out of his head. Living with him wasn't helping, but the thought of leaving sent a sharp pain through his stomach. He wished he knew someone who had some answers. Finally sleep came sometime in the middle of the night the way it had the last few days.

CHAPTER 5

"YOU LOOK awful," Emily said when he approached her desk.

"Thank you," Brian said sarcastically. "And you look like a pile of crap."

Emily grinned and looked down at her gray business suit. "That was exactly the look I was going for." She stood up from behind her desk. "Things can't be as bad as all that if you still have a sense of humor."

"Don't be so sure," Brian deadpanned.

Emily paused a second, assessing him. "Go into the conference room. Mrs. Maxwell will be in very soon."

Brian turned and entered the same large conference room where he'd met with Lydia previously. He slumped into a seat and closed his eyes, jumping slightly when the door closed.

"I'm going to go out on a limb and say that more than work has earned you the bags under your eyes." She slid an envelope across the desk. Brian didn't need to look inside. "Was there anything left from last week?"

"Ten dollars."

"That's good. You managed to feed yourself, and you found a job." Lydia looked him over. "You aren't dying, and you may look tired, but hard work will do that to you. Or did I guess right?"

"I don't fucking know," Brian swore. "I got a job mopping out showers and doing whatever they want me to do at a health club." He turned to her. "And yes, I've cleaned toilets. So what?" Brian put his arms over his chest, daring her to say something.

"Brian," his grandfather's voice said after a few seconds. He turned his attention to the now-familiar screen. "A person isn't measured by the job they hold or by how much they make. I quit school at sixteen. My first job was as a plumber's assistant, and I got in more shit—literally—than you could ever imagine. But I worked hard and learned. Being a plumber wasn't glamorous, but it helped my family. From there I learned the inside of homes and how they were put together. That taught me what builders needed, and I started Paulson Contracting. We started building homes and then branched out into developing products that contractors wanted to grow their businesses." The image of his grandfather smirked. "I bet my children and the rest of the family don't shout from the rooftops that the family business started with me cleaning up a load of crap."

The recording paused and then jumped ahead. Brian turned to Lydia.

"Your grandfather worked hard every day of his life."

"How did you meet him?" Brian asked.

"Your grandfather needed legal work after he was sued just after he started Paulson Contracting. He called my office, and we talked briefly. I answered my own phone, and he thought I was the secretary." Lydia's expression didn't waver. "When he arrived at my office, I explained who I was." Lydia grinned. "He took one look at me and laughed. I expected him to walk out of the meeting, but he listened and at the end said he'd see me in court. That was before women were thought of as anything other than nurses and telephone operators."

"Did you and my grandfather win?" Brian asked.

"You bet your ass we did, and I became your grandfather's attorney and have been for forty years." She looked up at the screen. "He was a great man, with the ability to see potential in others that most people miss."

Brian swallowed. "What if I want to bring this whole thing to an end and go back to my life? Can I do that?"

"Possibly." Lydia slowly swiveled her chair, a touch of fire in her eyes. "You can go back to living the life you had, but is that what you really want? Or only what you think is the easy way out of whatever, or whoever, is putting those bags under your eyes? The real question is what you really want. An easy life that means *nothing* to anyone at all, including you, or a little harder one that could mean everything."

"I wish I understood what was going on…," he muttered.

"You never will if you go back," Lydia told him. "We all have to find our own answers to some of life's questions. Your grandfather saw potential in me when I was basically fresh out of law school." She placed both hands on the table. "Do you think your grandfather would have gone to all this trouble if he hadn't seen something in you?" Lydia stood. "Find your own answers. Hard work means more than just doing your job. If you want something badly enough, you have to be willing to work for it… or him."

"But I don't know how to do the job right or get Cade," Brian said.

Lydia smiled. "I knew there was a guy. In the past you never engaged your heart. Maybe this young man who's captured your attention has also been able to reach something deeper that you've kept cut off." Lydia got up from her chair. "You can end this just by saying you want to."

"What will happen to the estate?" Brian asked.

"That won't be your concern. Your grandfather made provisions for every eventuality in his will. And it isn't my job to take sides as to how anything will come out. That's fully up to you, within the confines of your grandfather's wishes. But I think this is less about the will and more about you discovering what will make you happy." Lydia opened the conference room door. "I'll see you in a week."

She held the door, and Brian left the room, almost more confused than he'd been when he arrived.

"Brian," Lydia said quietly as he was about to leave the office. "Follow your heart."

She turned and went into her office, and Brian left, riding down in the elevator to the street, where he took the bus back toward Cade's apartment.

In the past, when Brian had been interested in someone, he'd wined and dined them. The finest restaurants in town, champagne, wine, shopping trips. He'd always used his money to get exactly what he wanted. But that wasn't an option now, and the one person he wanted more than he'd wanted anyone else in the past, was Cade. The problem was that he wasn't sure how to reach him. Brian didn't have the money to take him out to someplace fancy, and he was pretty sure that wasn't going to work with Cade anyway.

As he walked, Brian saw a florist shop and stopped, looking in the window. This was another way he'd used to get the attention he wanted. Most guys didn't get flowers, so Brian was sure to send them. That got noticed and was usually enough for him to get a date or two, followed by a few nights of passion. Brian left and continued on. There was no use looking at things he couldn't have or afford.

Brian ended up walking toward the health club and went inside to double-check his schedule for the week. He'd gotten used to getting up when most people were asleep, and he thought he was doing his job well enough.

Cade was working the desk. Brian shared a quick wave and a smile as he passed and hurried downstairs to the time clock area. He verified what times and days he was working and then went back upstairs. Peter was on his way in, and he grinned at Brian, but he didn't stop to talk, acting for all the world as though he were in a huge hurry. Brian thought of flipping him off, but instead he shrugged and kept going.

He was starting to get a much better picture of the people he'd had in his life. "Poser," he said under his breath before stopping at the desk on his way out. "Do you work at the restaurant tonight?" Brian asked Cade.

"No. I'm coming home, and I'm going to put my feet up." Cade looked drawn, and his eyes were half-lidded. The schedule he'd been keeping had to be catching up with him.

"Good. I'll see you then," Brian said, trying not to smile. He turned and left the club. He could have walked to the apartment, but he turned the other way and ended up at the grocery store. People bustled in and out, and Brian went through the automatic doors, wondering what he should do. He had pretty much decided to try to make something for dinner on the walk over, but his cooking abilities were so limited that he didn't know where to start. He knew of only one person who might be able to help.

"Maria," he said. "Thank you for answering my call."

"Mr. Brian?" she said. "I not supposed to talk to you. They say I keep my job if I no see you."

"Well, you can't see me. You're only talking to me, and I need help. There's someone I like, and I want to make dinner for him, but I don't know how to cook anything. Can you tell me what I should do?"

Her response was to laugh. "What do you want to make him?"

"I don't know. Something easy, because I'm a really bad cook, but I want it to be nice."

"Pasta is easy, and you can start with awful jar sauce and add things to make it better. That's what I do. You can add some garlic and maybe oregano until it taste good. Buy garlic bread, and you have a nice meal that you can cook if you lucky." She was clearly having fun with this. "I must go, but good luck."

She hung up, and Brian sighed. At least he had a game plan.

That is, until he got into the pasta aisle and tried to figure out what to get. He closed his eyes and ended up with the pasta shaped like bow ties. Then he went to the sauce section and was equally confused. Once again he pretty much closed his eyes and grabbed a jar, as long as it didn't have mushrooms. Brian hated food with fungi. Then he got the garlic bread and hurried to the checkout. After he paid, he walked to the apartment.

"COOKING A meal shouldn't be this complicated," Brian said out loud to the empty apartment as he read the instructions for each component. Not that anything was particularly complicated, but he wanted them all to come out at the same time. Once he figured it out, Brian realized he was hours too early to start anything and ended up watching some afternoon television, which was ghastly. Where in heck did they come up with this torture? It was funny, but at home, he was always busy. If he needed something fun, he called friends and went out. Of course, now that he thought about it, they were always ready to go, probably because Brian was willing to pull out his credit card. How could he have been so stupid? He'd had fun, and he'd been the big man in the group, but that was only to pay for things.

A sharp knock on the door pulled him out of his morose thoughts. Brian opened it, surprised to see Cade's mother and brother.

"I tried calling Cade, but his phone keeps going straight to voice mail." She sounded frantic. "My boss called, and I have to go in. I know it's last minute, and I was hoping Cade was home, but could you watch Phillip for a few hours?"

Brian nodded and motioned for him to come in. "Of course. We can keep each other company. Cade is still working, but he'll be home in a few hours."

Brian tried to remember where Cade kept the art supplies, but it seemed Phillip knew, and he was already pulling them out by the time his mother had said good-bye and was on her way out. Brian wanted to ask her what she'd have done if he hadn't been here, but that was none of his business, and she was clearly frantic, wondering what she was going to do.

"You draw too?" Phillip said.

Brian locked the door and joined Phillip at the table. "Are you hungry?" Brian asked, but he got no answer. Phillip was engrossed in what he was doing, so Brian moved to the living room and sat on the sofa to watch television. After about an hour, Phillip lost interest and joined him. Brian let Phillip choose what he wanted to watch.

"*Star Wars,*" Phillip said and pulled out the DVD.

Brian put it in, and he was transported back to the seventies. He'd seen this movie more times than he could count and knew half the dialogue, cheesy as it was, by heart. Phillip was enthralled, and Brian got some snacks that they both ate without taking their eyes off the screen.

"What's going on here?" Cade said when he came in.

"Your mother was in a bind, so Phillip and I are watching guy movies." He was just happy that Phillip hadn't wanted to watch *Toy Story* again. "Sorry if we made a little mess."

"What's all this?" Cade asked as he went into the kitchen area.

"Darn," he groaned, remembering his original plans. "I was going to try to make you dinner… and things got a little off track." Brian got off the sofa and joined Cade. "Go on and sit with your brother. I'm going to try cooking. I promise I'll ask for help if it looks like I'm going to poison anyone."

The smile Cade gave him lit the room. "You have no idea…."

The thing was that Brian did understand how Cade felt. Maybe not the full reason behind it, but he understood someone doing something nice for him. Cade had been kind to him in a way few people were, so doing something to make him happy was special—surprisingly special. "Just show me where the pots are, and I'll get started."

Cade opened the cupboard, and Brian got the pot he needed and filled it with water. Brian shooed Cade out of the kitchen and got to work as best he could. It took him time to find everything, and he had to be careful not to dump the entire bottle of oregano into the sauce, but all in all he muddled through, making his first

70

dinner ever without too many headaches or mishaps. He ended up cooking the entire package of pasta, which seemed about right with three people.

"This is good," Phillip pronounced with his first bite and continued eating.

"I hoped it would be edible, but I didn't expect raves," Brian said before taking his first bite.

"It's good." Cade reached over the table and put his hand on Brian's. "I really appreciate you making dinner and watching Phillip for Mom. It's a big help."

It was the least he could do. "Don't expect me to cook much more. Otherwise we'll be eating a lot of pasta. Apparently it's all I can make."

"You did very well."

Cade took a piece of the slightly singed garlic bread and cut off the dark part before eating it with relish. Brian did the same and thought the bread was okay. He should have cooked it less and maybe added a little more butter. Still, he was hungry and dug into the meal. Once they were done, Cade did the dishes, and they all settled on the sofa to watch the rest of *Star Wars*.

The movie was ending when Shirley returned to pick up Phillip. He'd been half asleep on the sofa, so he went quietly with his mother, who thanked Brian for saving her, and then they both left. Once the door closed, Cade flopped down on the sofa with a slight huff.

"I'm starting to get worried."

"Why?"

"I see how tired Mom is. Phillip is great, but he requires constant care and supervision. She loves him and will do anything for Phillip, but I'm afraid she's working herself to death." Cade pulled one of the sofa pillows over his chest, hugging it to himself. "I'm trying to do what I can to help."

"But there's only so much you can do."

"Yeah," Cade breathed as Brian sat down next to him.

"You're a good person," Brian said softly. He knew he wasn't and never had been. Self-centered and self-absorbed were some of the nicest terms he could use to describe himself. Others might have said he was generous because he paid for things, but that was just so he could be the center of attention. And look what that had gotten him—friends who weren't really friends and a life that ended up as lonely as he'd always feared he was going to be.

"We do what we have to, Brian. Phillip and Mom need me, so I do what I can. They're my family." He said that as though those few words explained everything.

Brian shook his head slowly. "You should meet my family. They wouldn't walk across the street for each other. They form these alliances in order to get what they want and then screw each other over when they want something else. We're like a pack of ravenous dogs that'll band together and then eat each other when it suits. The only thing that holds anyone together is my grandfather's money. They can all agree on one thing, that they want control of as much of that as possible." Brian was so fed up with them, he could scream. Instead he closed his eyes and rested his head on Cade's shoulder. "I'm sick of all of them."

"My family has nothing…."

"And yet you work hard to help each other. My family has everything…."

"And they couldn't care less about each other."

"Exactly," Brian said. "They all brag about what they do to help other people. They serve on boards and hold charity events, but they never actually touch any of the people they help. That might get them dirty or something." Brian was beginning to see a lot of things his family was doing wrong. Not that he was particularly surprised. The question was, what should they be doing? Brian didn't have the answer to that.

"Sometimes it isn't the family you're born with that counts," Cade said.

Brian wasn't sure what he meant.

"Sometimes gay guys like us get rejected by our families, and they make their own family of close friends. It happens all the time. So if you want, you can just build your own family."

"I wish it was that easy," Brian said. "I thought I had good friends, but it turned out…. Let's just say when the going got tough, they bailed fast."

"Not everyone bailed," Cade whispered, and Brian lifted his head and turned toward Cade, lightly touching his chin as he kissed him.

Heat bloomed through Brian like an instant inferno. He shifted on the sofa, turning toward Cade, deepening the kiss as he shifted his weight, pressing Cade back on the cushions. He tasted good, and the little moaning sounds were like Viagra. He ached inside and wound his arms around Cade, desperate to hold him tight.

"Brian," Cade groaned, patting him on the shoulder. "We need to take things slower."

His eyes were huge and shining, the most gorgeous thing Brian had ever seen. Brian swore he could almost hear his heart beating.

"I…."

He was breathing hard, and Brian backed away so Cade could sit back up.

"Things don't work out for me in the boyfriend department."

"I find that hard to believe," Brian said, running his fingers through Cade's silky blond hair. "You have to have a lot of guys interested in you."

Cade shook his head. "There's where you'd be wrong. I've had a few boyfriends who all bailed—half of them when they met Phillip and couldn't deal with him. I learned if they were these really smooth guys, perfect in every way, they couldn't take being around someone who wasn't perfect. The rest wanted more than I could give them. They didn't understand why my family and Phillip had to come first, so they ended up leaving after not very long. One guy professed his love but was gone within a week."

"Sounds like a real prince," Brian said sarcastically.

"It was his bit. He told guys he loved them so they would sleep with him. He was just a horndog. Thankfully I didn't sleep with him, but my friend Gene did once." Cade grinned. "Gene said I wasn't missing anything. Gene said he was like sleeping with a half-dead fish. He expected to be worshipped or something and just lay there."

"Well, that's really attractive and just what everyone wants." Brian tugged Cade to him. "I can wait, if that's what you want." He quivered anyway and hoped Cade hadn't felt it. His heart pounded faster and faster as he was wrapped in Cade's intoxicating scent. He wanted nothing more than to pick Cade up in his arms and carry him to the bed, caveman style if necessary. His head swam in a sea of hormones and endorphins, but somehow he kept his control and pulled away, breathing hard until his mind cleared of its haze of lust. Cade deserved better treatment than a quick romp on the sofa.

Brian stood and walked across the room, needing some distance. He'd never felt so singularly determined before. It was like he was a cat and Cade the world's strongest catnip, or Brian-nip in this case.

"It isn't as though I've had good luck in the boyfriend pursuits either."

"You? I bet guys throw themselves at you all the time," Cade said. "All you have to do is crook your finger, and they'll come running."

"Maybe, but why are they running? Is it because they're interested in me or what I can get for them? My grandmother always said to be careful and make sure people liked me for me. I tried to do that with boyfriends, but I should have taken that to heart with everyone." He was such an idiot.

Cade stood, looking a little wobbly on his legs. "I'm going to go to bed. We need to go in to work early in the morning."

Cade turned away, and Brian jumped up, wrapping Cade in his arms before he could get too far away.

"I'm not asking for anything you aren't ready for. But you don't need to rush away."

Cade turned in his arms. "Yes, I do. If we stay like this, I'm not going to be able to think straight, and we'll end up doing something that we may wish we hadn't."

Cade trembled slightly. The movement was almost too subtle, but Brian knew what it was, and his heart leapt. He leaned close, kissing Cade once again, this time letting his need flow through his lips to Cade. Then, when he couldn't hold his breath any longer, he broke the kiss and pulled away. He watched Cade go to his room and then returned to make up the sofa for the night. One thing Brian knew, working early or not, sleep was going to be difficult.

DAYS TURNED into weeks, and Brian slowly settled into his new routine. What surprised him most about this new—or temporary—life was that he liked the routine and having to be somewhere each day. He also liked that when he was at the apartment, at least part of the time Cade was there, and for the most part his old life had kept its distance.

That was, until the end of June.

"Brian," his uncle snapped when he answered the phone.

"Hold on a minute," Brian said with a slight surge of delight while he checked in a member who had forgotten their card. "Thank you," he called brightly and then returned to the phone. "I'm back."

"Where are you?" his uncle asked, and Brian ignored his question.

"You called for a reason?" Brian reminded him.

"Yes. The family got together and decided that the barbeque Dad always had on the Fourth should continue, so I'm holding it at my house. I sent an invitation but didn't get a response, so I figured I'd call." He made it sound like such a chore.

"All right. What time?"

"The party will start at three and run through the evening fireworks on the lake. So I can put you down for one?"

"Two," Brian said. He saw another member coming in. "I have to go, but thank you for the call and the invitation." He hung up and checked in the member with a smile that lasted until the woman was out of sight. Why did any dealings with his family have the effect of pulling the fun out of everything like some giant vacuum cleaner that was determined to make the world as miserable as they were? Brian wished he'd said he was busy.

"Thanks for manning the desk," Cade said when he came up the stairs from his lunch break.

"No problem." He waited for Cade to join him. "Do you have to work at Bartolome's on the Fourth?"

"No. I think it's my one holiday off this year. Why?"

"Do you want to go to a picnic? We can leave after work. It's at my uncle's. There will be lots of food, and you'll be doing me a huge favor."

"You want me to meet your family?" Cade asked as though it were a huge deal.

Brian wanted to kick himself. "They're no prize, believe me. But it would be nice to have a date. The house has a great view of the fireworks, and it's right on the lake. There's also a pool, so we can go swimming if you like." Maybe he shouldn't be selling this idea so hard. "Cade, I'd really like it if you'd come with me," he finally said once he got his mouth under control. "It would make the day nicer."

Cade chuckled. "Dang, they must be something else if an invitation can have you selling so hard and running off at the mouth."

Great, Cade was teasing him. He hoped that was a good sign.

"I think it could be fun to see these people. You've talked about them enough that you've got my curiosity up. Heck, I expect half of them to have horns."

BRIAN WAS nervous as the Fourth got closer. Things had been going so well with Cade. They hadn't progressed beyond kissing, but some of the make-out sessions they'd had were pretty hot. Cade seemed content to take things slow, and Brian wasn't going to push it. He could control himself, and getting to know Cade was turning out to be an adventure in itself.

The worst part was calling Lydia. "I've been invited to my uncle's for the holiday."

"That's very good. Your grandfather did say that family was important."

Brian rolled his eyes. "It's more like a command performance. Cade is going to go with me."

They chatted for a few more minutes, and then Brian hung up so he could check the bus schedules. He found that buses ran sporadically to that section of town, although once the fireworks let out, getting home on the bus could take hours with the traffic.

After working at the club the next day, they went back to Cade's apartment to change and then took the bus to his uncle's. As they got closer, Brian began to rethink his plan. Maybe bringing Cade to the cookout wasn't the greatest idea.

"Why are you nervous?" Cade asked.

"I'm wondering about this whole idea," he said honestly.

Cade's smile fell. "I'll do my best not to embarrass you." He turned away, his leg bouncing up and down.

"I didn't mean that. I'm concerned that they treat you nicely." Brian hadn't paid much attention to how Cade was dressed, but his family would definitely take in the ordinary clothes and the worn bag that held Cade's swimming gear. He'd gotten the clothes and his bathing suit at Goodwill, but he could take whatever his family threw at him. "I'm glad you came with me, and I want you to have a good time."

"Oh." Cade's lips curled upward nervously as he looked down at his clothes. "Do you think someone will say something?"

"No." Brian sure hoped they didn't. Though his aunt in particular had made the thinly veiled, backhanded insult an art form. They wouldn't say anything to Cade's face, but they would talk about him when he wasn't around. It was too late to change his mind, but Brian was definitely wishing he hadn't put them in this position. He wasn't going to hurt Cade by not taking him. "We'll have a really good time." He hoped he was right.

Cade whistled when they walked up the drive of his uncle's Tudor pile of a house. "This is huge. Was it built in the twenties?" Cade asked half breathlessly. "I've been down Lake Drive lots of times, but this is the first time I'll get to go inside one of these houses."

His eyes were huge, and Brian smiled slightly, glad that Cade was excited.

Brian led Cade through the house to the backyard. There were dozens of people. Most of them Brian knew, but some were strangers to him. Not that it mattered. The kids were in and around the pool, playing loudly and laughing. Guests were seated in various groups around a large central patio. Food was on tables with billowing tablecloths on the lawn, and of course a bar had been set up, complete with bartender. Nothing was ever left to chance, and his uncle always went all out to make a good impression.

"Brian," his uncle said, shaking his hand and then turning to Cade. "Who's your friend?"

"This is Cade McAllister," he said. "My uncle, Harry Paulson."

They shook hands tentatively.

"McAllister, I don't think I know any McAllisters. What line of work is your family in?"

He seemed interested, but Brian was wary.

"Restaurants," Cade said, and Brian smiled and nodded.

"We have interests in a number of restaurant chains," Uncle Harry said. "Are any of your family chefs? Is there anyone I might know?"

His uncle was fishing, and Brian saw him looking Cade over the way a wolf sniffs its meal before devouring it.

"Cade, we can put our bags in the pool house, and then there are some people I'd like you to meet." Brian smiled at his uncle. "Is that the Seligs?" Brian asked to draw his uncle's attention. He knew his uncle would consider the former commissioner of baseball more important than he was. It didn't hurt that they had just arrived, and sure enough his uncle hurried over to greet them, and Brian was able to make an escape with Cade.

"Are you ashamed of me?" Cade asked. "I don't care if your uncle knows I work as a waiter. It's what I do, not who I am." Cade stopped at the edge of the pool. "This is your family, and they are who they are. I'm here to have a good time and because you asked me. I don't really care what they think of me."

"I really don't care either," Brian agreed.

"I think you do. For whatever reason you want them to like you, and that's why you're worried."

Cade turned and began walking back the way they'd come. Brian wondered where he was going and after a second hurried to catch up with him.

"It's okay, Brian. Everyone wants to be liked. It's not a sin."

"Dammit," Brian breathed under his breath, berating himself. "Can we just have fun?" he asked Cade.

"Yeah," he said, handing Brian his bag. "Will you go take care of this? I'll get us something to drink."

Cade turned away, and Brian wondered if he'd been forgiven or not. Brian went and put the bags in the pool house, dodging running and dripping kids and navigating the scattered pool chairs. He said hello to people as he went and finally got the bags where they needed to go.

"Hey, Brian," Courtney Neveral said from where she lay in the sun, draped across the lounger in what had to be the smallest pink bikini known to man, so spring was busting out all over. Not that she had anything that interested him. "It's been a while." She patted the chair next to hers. "I heard about your troubles. I'm sure it's only temporary." She batted her eyelashes, trying to be alluring, but it came off as desperate.

"Courtney," Brian began, about to dash her hopes, when Cade approached with a glass filled with something pink in each hand.

"Hey, Brian, I wasn't sure what you wanted, and they recommended this." Cade grinned. "It's really yummy." He handed Brian a glass and stepped closer, staring at Courtney and then turning quizzically to Brian.

"Courtney, this is Cade. He and I have been seeing each other for a few weeks now."

"I've seen you," Cade said. "You always look so fabulous when you come into the restaurant." He sipped his drink, and Courtney primped like a hen straightening her feathers.

"I'm sorry…," she said quizzically, seemingly trying to place Cade. "Oh, you're the server from Bartolome's."

Brian braced for a snide comment, but her smile got bigger.

"You saved me last week when my klutz of a boyfriend spilled wine." She turned to Brian. "He was right there and kept me from getting wine on my dress. He even helped me up and away from the table." She looked at the two of them. "You make a cute couple." She stuck her lower lip out. "The cute ones are always gay or married… sometimes both." She sat up. "Join me."

Brian brought over a second chair and joined the two of them. "Sweetheart, I have to ask…," Cade was saying as he returned. "Are the girls real? Because if they are, you were blessed by the gods themselves."

Courtney giggled. "Yeah. I hate needles and knives. Could never voluntarily have surgery." She shook dramatically and leaned closer to Cade. "I thought about having my nose done once and chickened out."

"Don't do anything," Cade said. "People look best the way they were made." He sipped from his glass. "So do you have a boyfriend?"

"No. I dumped the klutz. When he wasn't spilling things, his idea of having a good time was staying at home, drinking beer, and eating God knows what, and watching football. I like to go out and want a guy to have some fun with. Sitting at home is fine, but I want someone to pay attention to me every once in a while."

"Klutz didn't do that?" Cade asked, and Brian realized he was charming Courtney to no end.

"Once I put on one of his football jerseys and nothing else. I walked into the room while he was watching a game, and he told me I was blocking the television."

She shook her head, and Cade rolled his eyes. Brian didn't know what to make of these two, so he just sat back to listen.

"I knew then he wasn't worth the effort."

"Do you ever come in to the Downtown Health Club? I know quite a few of the guys there, and I can introduce you to some of the nicer ones. Do you like older guys?" Cade turned to Brian. "Mason, the guy who comes in every day at six? He's really nice."

"Six… in the morning?" she asked, completely taken aback.

"Yeah. He comes in a mess before work and leaves the club looking like he walked out of the pages of GQ. I'm not sure where he works, but the man has style." Cade leaned closer. "He had this awful girlfriend a year ago, and she cheated on him. He's dated some, and he came in with a girl once, but I think he's looking to settle down." Cade pulled out his wallet. "Here's a guest pass. Stop in, and I'll introduce you."

She took the card like it was the ticket to heaven.

"I have the worst luck with guys."

"That's why you need friends. To help weed out the thistles and find the ones who'll bring roses."

Courtney flashed her million-watt smile, the one that left most men speechless and stuttering. "I like that. You're a real sweetheart."

Cade was clearly soaking up what Courtney was saying, and it seemed the two of them had become fast friends. "Would you like a drink?" Brian asked Courtney. She asked for champagne, and he got up to get some, emptying his glass into one of the beds. The drink was way too sweet and fruity for him, but he wasn't going to tell Cade.

"I see you deigned to show up," his aunt said when she cornered Brian as he waited for the bartender. It was a hot day, and the bar was popular. She, on the other hand, looked like her last drink had a little too much lemon.

"I see your disposition hasn't improved. You know, if you'd smile and maybe have a little fun, the lines on your face would fade, and you'd be much more pleasant." He leaned close like he was going to share a secret. "If you get any more severe, you'll bring storm clouds with you." He smiled when she glanced upward.

"You always thought you knew better than everyone else. Your mother thought the same thing, and look what happened to her. She had to be better than everyone else, and it cost her everything."

The venom took Brian by surprise.

"She was always Daddy's favorite. They used to spend hours and days together working on his pet projects. Daddy always listened to her to the detriment of everyone else."

This was all news to him. Of course, information from his aunt was always to be taken with a pound of salt. "They worked closely together."

"Yes. Because of her, he built the wing onto the children's hospital and gave all that money to the art museum. That money could have been put to work for the family, but she got him to just give it away."

"But...." He paused, trying to fathom what she was saying. "You spend hours with your charities and are always hosting benefits." That made no sense.

"Of course I do, but I don't give them all my money." She hissed softly so no one around could hear and rolled her eyes like she was making all the sense in the world.

He reached the front of the line and asked for a tequila and tonic and some champagne for Courtney. "It's always good talking to you," he said to his aunt when he took the drinks. "Like a ray of sunshine," he added sarcastically and walked to where he'd left Cade.

He was surrounded by women, all of whom had pulled up chairs and were gathered around him. "Do you think you can find me someone nice?" Heather Beaman was asking.

"It's about where you're looking. Good men who want to settle down don't frequent clubs and bars. They go to church or go to, believe it or not, PTA meetings. They have kids and are trying to rebuild their families. It isn't so much the men you're meeting as where you're meeting them."

"How do you know so much?" Heather asked.

"Because," Cade began with a grin, "I'm a man, and I also date them. Who better to know what guys want and where to find them?"

He looked up at Brian, completely adorable, and Brian's mouth went Sahara dry. Brian wanted him so bad in that moment.

"Right, Brian?"

He shook his head. "Don't ask me. Until lately I haven't had any luck with men."

"Until lately. What have you been doing differently?" Cade asked, and the others around them seemed to slide into the background for just a few seconds. "Maybe you were looking in different places, or maybe you decided to get to know the guy before you jumped into bed with him. After all, what's the allure if you give away the milk for free?" Cade glanced at the ladies around him. "Most men are horndogs. If we can get sex, we will. Heck, men want three things more than anything: sex, food, and television. Most guys would be in heaven if they could have all three at the same time."

"How would that work?" Brian asked without looking away from Cade.

"Not that I've given it much thought but a guy eating fried chicken and having sex on the floor while watching the television, would probably think he won the man lottery." Cade turned to the ladies. "So the way to a man's heart is through his stomach, most definitely. And don't give him everything he wants up front. Build the anticipation, and make him woo you a little."

"Woo?" Courtney asked, and Brian could almost see all the women taking mental notes.

"Yeah. Take you to dinner, flowers. If he's worth having, then he should make an effort to win your affection." Cade met Heather's normally steely gaze, which was now as warm as melted butter. "You should also make an effort to make an impression on him."

"How do we do that?" one of the other ladies asked.

"Melissa, you need to take an interest in something that's important to him. I'm not saying you need to go hunting, but find something he likes to do. Watch action flicks with him. See, he'll watch your movies because he wants sex or hopes there will be sex at some time in the future."

"Okay," Melissa said.

"And one other thing. When you get angry at your man, you give him the silent treatment, right?"

The women nodded in near unison.

"Guys don't get that at all. You're leaving them alone to watch television, and it's quiet." Cade shrugged. "It isn't a punishment."

"Then what do we do?"

"Don't play games. Talk to him. Guys really like that." Cade grinned once again.

"I think that's enough of you giving away all our secrets," Brian teased, and Cade stood from the lounger where he'd been holding court. Most straight men would give their eyeteeth to be the center of so much female attention. In a way, Brian was jealous. Cade had captured all those people's attention simply by virtue of his personality and kind nature. Brian had always gotten attention because he'd paid for things. But even Courtney had been interested in Cade and hung on everything he said.

Cade said good-bye with a huge smile and carried his glass as they moved through groups of milling people. "They were so nice."

"They are." Brian looked around, wondering why he'd felt this need to pull Cade away from the people he was talking to. The truth was, if he looked deeply, he wanted Cade's attention for himself. "Did you mean what you said, or what you sort of said?"

"Yeah," Cade answered and sipped from his glass. "I think maybe my luck is changing, or I hope it might be changing."

"With me?" Brian wanted to be clear. He hoped there wasn't someone else, but he wasn't trusting his judgment at the moment. Things in his life weren't nearly as clear as they'd always seemed, and he wasn't totally certain he was picking up on things he should.

"Yes, dummy." Cade grinned and chuckled. "Phillip loves you. After you watched him, he called and asked if he could come over and color with Brian again. Phillip has an innate sense for good people, and if he likes you, then that says a lot."

"Brian," his aunt interrupted, more shrilly than necessary. He tensed. "Who's your friend?" She softened her tone when others seemed to notice her.

"Aunt Jean, this is Cade." Brian purposely gave her no additional information.

"It's a pleasure to meet you," Cade said as he extended his hand.

His aunt hesitated and then shook it lightly.

"Likewise." She pulled back her hand, clamping them both around her glass. "What is it you do?" Jean asked, and Brian stifled a groan. *Let the inquisition begin.*

"I'm a waiter at Bartolome's," Cade answered directly.

"Oh," she half breathed, barely forming the words.

Brian tensed as he felt his aunt's snob-meter rise.

"How did you meet?"

"I was on my way to work, and a man in the park tried to mug me. Brian stopped him, and from there our paths kept crossing."

Cade glanced at him, and Brian tried to think of a way to extricate Cade.

"He's a very nice person."

His aunt scoffed. "None of us are particularly nice people. If we were, we wouldn't have any money left." She chuckled with a slightly superior air.

"I don't know about that," Cade said.

"Believe me, we may seem nice on the outside."

Brian stifled a scoff. He hadn't seen many demonstrations of his family's outward niceness. Then again, he supposed his aunt might consider her charity work as being nice.

"But underneath it's a completely different story."

His uncle Harry joined them with his wife, Brian's aunt Gaby, in tow.

"Are you having a nice time?" Aunt Gaby asked with her usual bright smile.

He wondered how she had ended up with his uncle. Aunt Gaby was generally nice but very quiet.

"Cade is a waiter," Aunt Jean said with an undertone that set Brian's spine on edge.

Cade shrugged, and Brian wanted to punch her.

"Where do you work?" Aunt Gaby asked.

"I started at Bartolome's a few weeks ago. They treat us very well, and it's a nice place to work." Cade either hadn't caught his aunt's tone or chose to ignore it.

"You all have a good time," his uncle said with more graciousness than Brian had ever thought he was capable of.

"Thank you," Cade said brightly, and Courtney motioned to Cade, who excused himself and walked back toward where she waited for him.

"Brian," his uncle said as soon as Cade was out of earshot. "I know you think you're gay, and if that's the way you want to live your life, then so be it. But you could find someone of higher… shall we say, caliber."

"Harry," Aunt Gaby snapped, and Brian and his aunt turned to her in surprise. In all his life Brian had never heard her use that tone before. "That's a terrible thing to say." She glared at him and then turned away, walking straight across the patio and into the house. His uncle sighed and watched her go for a second.

"I'm serious. You need to be careful to make sure he isn't after your money." He leaned closer. "I have an investigator if you decide you're serious about this person."

"Exactly," Brian's other aunt said. "Now that you can get married." Her lip curled upward. "I really don't understand the need for that."

"It's called equality," Brian said.

"Please. People are never equal."

She whirled around and called out to some friend of her friends. Brian shook his head and turned back to his uncle.

"I'm serious. If you're looking for some fun, a guy like that is all right, but if you really want to bring another man into the family, then you need to make sure he has some substance. Not a waiter." He sounded as though he were making a royal pronouncement.

Brian had had enough, but he managed to hold his tongue. Cade's warm laugh drifted across to his ears, and Brian turned away without acknowledging his uncle. Brian intended to walk over to Cade, but instead he turned away and headed down the path to the beach. He needed a few minutes to think.

"Brian," Cade called, and Brian stopped and waited for him to catch up. "What's wrong?"

Brian turned, looking up the bluff. "My fucking family."

"I don't care what they say about me. You have to know that. They have all this, and I live in a tiny apartment and make my living waiting tables. I'll never have anything like this, and it doesn't matter. They can say whatever they want."

"But…." Brian turned from where he'd been staring at the water. He scooped up a rock and heaved it as far into the lake as he could. "I think like them…."

Cade touched his arm. "Do you really?"

"Of course I do. I grew up with those people, and I spent years with them learning to think and act like them. All my friends raced for the hills when they found out I wasn't going to be able to pay for things any longer. That crap went on for years, and I was either too stupid or too blind to see it." He grabbed a rock and then another, each thunking into the water. He wanted to throw himself in after them.

"You can change if you want to," Cade said.

"Really? I can change like that? I've spent years getting everything I ever wanted. Money was no object. Cars, meals, drinks, people, anything. And I'm supposed to walk away from that and be like everyone else." Brian turned toward Cade, who glared daggers at him.

"So the time you've spent with Phillip and me has been an act? You were so good with him, and I've seen happiness and even laughter in the last few weeks. Was that part of some sort of scheme?" Cade stepped closer.

"Of course not," Brian protested.

"Then quit being an ass. You're a person the same as they are, and you have the ability to choose the type of guy you want to be. And don't tell me you want to be like them. If you did, then you'd be in seventh heaven and you never would have asked me to come with you. Instead you're angry with your family and completely miserable because you aren't happy and haven't been in a long time."

Brian wanted to rail at Cade, but the truth was staring him in the face, and he wasn't in the mood to lie. "So you think you know me." Deflecting was easier.

"I know enough. You paid for everything and had a large group of friends because they were easy. You paid, and they stayed in line, never questioning you or challenging anything. You had your nice little box of apathy and stayed there. Now you're questioning it. That alone says you're more than they are. The question is whether you want to go back and become your own person." Cade turned and began walking away. "I'm going to rejoin the party."

Brian watched Cade go. "What do I do?"

Cade stopped and waited. Brian sighed and walked toward him to the path up the bluff.

"That's up to you. No one can answer that question for you. We all have to decide the person we're going to be."

Brian looked up to the house. "So my aunt and uncle decided to be asses."

Cade laughed. "No. Your aunt and uncle decided to make money and position the most important things in their lives, and now they can't get enough of either."

"How do you know this after meeting them for five minutes?"

"Am I wrong?" Cade asked, and Brian couldn't say no. "But they don't matter. You do. They have no control over you, and yet you worry what they think. I don't give a pile of crap for their opinion, so they can't hurt me." Cade began walking again.

Brian wanted to go home. And in a second he realized he meant back to Cade's. This party wasn't all that interesting, and why spend more time with these people who were supposed to be his family? "Do you want to go?"

"We can if you want to," Cade said. "But not all of the people here are like your family. Some of them are pretty nice. So choose the people you talk to and stay away from the rest."

Cade held out his hand, and Brian stared at it before entwining his fingers with Cade's.

"Be your own man."

"I don't think I know how," Brian said honestly.

"Sure you do. You got your own job and are making your way. That's what my mom told me being your own man was."

They climbed the bluff and entered the yard at the top. Brian tried to release Cade's hand, but Cade held on, and when their eyes met, Brian entwined his fingers once again just as he caught his uncle's eye and the scowl that formed on his lips. Brian turned away, and they crossed the yard to the pool, where Courtney was chatting with a group of guys.

"Cade," she called with a smile. "I was telling these guys about you." She got up and hurried over, grabbed his free hand and hauled them both into the group.

"You were?"

Brian leaned close. "Courtney has dated most of these guys at one time or another."

"Huh," Cade said. "So this is the gathering of the exes."

Courtney giggled. "Yeah, I guess."

Cade leaned a little closer to her. "Which one is the klutz?"

Courtney shifted her gaze and flicked it back to them.

"So what's going on?" Skip asked.

He was one of the biggest guys Brian knew and always had the world's most vacant expression. Nice house, nobody home... ever.

"Are you into this whole... metrosexual thing?"

Brian raised his eyebrows. If asked, he would have doubted Skip knew what metrosexual was. Though sex was probably Skip's one skill, if rumor was correct.

"Please. This is Brian's boyfriend. He's nice and a lot more interesting to talk to than you ever were. After all, he thinks with his big head rather than with what's between his legs."

She giggled, and Brian gave her credit for more brains than he'd thought.

"You need to find a boyfriend with a mind," Cade told Courtney.

"They don't have anything on this," Skip boasted and flexed his arms. Then he did a little hip thrust to draw attention to what was most likely a considerable endowment. Not that Brian was particularly interested.

"Please. You spend most of your time thinking about sports. Smart guys think about sex… a lot. And we're usually more generous. After all, we may not have his kind of bait"—Cade thumbed in Skip's direction—"but after a few months we can hold a conversation."

"He's just teasing you," Brian interjected when it looked as though the top of Skip's head was going to fly off.

"I don't like it."

"You don't like anything other than fast cars and sex," Courtney commented.

Skip made some sort of grunt and then turned away in search of others on whom he could work his charms. Cade pulled up chairs, and they all settled in for a while.

BRIAN STAYED away from his aunt and uncle for most of the rest of the day. Uncle Harry used the party as a chance to schmooze, and he seemed pretty good at it. Brian's aunt Jean eventually sank into a chair somewhere and proceeded to drown her sorrows, but not her sharp tongue, in plenty of wine.

"Are you getting hungry?" Cade asked, and they took a turn through the sumptuous buffet designed to impress.

Who had caviar at a cookout anyway? Not that it mattered. Cade was happy, and to Brian's amusement, he was as well. These parties were usually stuffy and dull. Cade had made this one fun just by being his warm, bubbly self. Nearly everyone stopped by at some point, and Cade seemed to charm almost all of them. A few times Brian wondered if it was because some people actually wanted to see if he'd brought a waiter to the party. But nearly one and all left charmed and with a smile on their face.

Once darkness fell, the anticipation built, and people moved their chairs to the edge of the bluff, looking toward downtown. A few, like Aunt Jean, had had too much to drink. His aunt sat in a chair with her head back, glass in hand. Brian wondered a few times if she'd passed out. He happened to be watching her as the first firework streaked into the air. She jumped to her feet, spilling her drink on her Jimmy Choos.

Cade nudged him, and Brian turned away as the fireworks exploded in the sky. Fountains of red, blue, green, and white fire lit the atmosphere. The best part of the show was the way Cade glided closer, leaning against him, arms entwined. People *ooo*'d and *ahh*'d a little around them, but Brian didn't really hear it. Cade took up his entire attention, through the first shell to the rousing middle and the booming finale that sent color shooting high into the sky and waves of sound crashing over all of them.

Suddenly all went quiet as the echoes died away. The bubble around the two of them stayed in place for a few minutes, and then the jostling and conversations began once again.

"I think we can go now," Brian whispered to Cade, who nodded. They said their good-byes, and thankfully his uncle was too busy for more than a few words. They walked to the bus stop and caught it just in time. Heavy traffic clogged the street, thousands of people trying to get home from the fireworks.

They got off the bus a few stops early and walked the rest of the way. Brian stopped on the sidewalk outside the front door, looking up at the building.

"What is it?" Cade asked before moving toward the door.

"I don't know," Brian answered honestly without looking away.

Cade returned and took his arm, leading him down the sidewalk. "What are you thinking about?"

"The fact that I've lived in houses as big as my uncle's or fancy places like at Cudahy Tower all my life. And your tiny apartment with me sleeping on the couch seems more like home than any of them have in a long time. I wish I knew why." Brian held Cade's arm as they walked. Cade didn't say anything as he led him farther from the apartment. "Where are we going?"

"Just around the block." Cade continued leading him, letting Brian think and walk. When they reached the front door of the building again, Cade unlocked it, and they went inside, climbed the stairs, and walked into Cade's apartment.

The door closed, and Brian turned to Cade without saying a word. He knew what he wanted more than anything in his life at that moment. Cade stared back, and Brian held his hands at his sides, leaning forward and holding still.

Cade closed the distance between them, and as soon as their lips touched, Brian pulled Cade to him, holding him tight as he deepened the kiss. The room was dark, but Brian had spent enough time here to know his way around.

He slipped his hand under Cade's shirt, palm pressing to his chest, propelling him backward toward the bedroom, stopping at the door. "Is this what you want?" Brian whispered.

"Yes," Cade groaned. "I have since that first night you stayed here."

Brian stiffened and looked for a hint of exaggeration.

"I spent most of the night listening for footsteps and hoping for a knock on the door. Scared it might happen at the same time because I knew I should say no but didn't want to." Cade reached behind himself and opened the door, backing inside with Brian keeping up, kissing him the entire way to the bed.

Brian followed Cade down onto the bed, instinct and need taking over for reason. He knew what he wanted, and Cade had been calling to him all day. It was funny, he'd been to parties with other people and always ended up looking for them at one point, but all day he'd known exactly where Cade was out of sheer instinct.

He tugged at the hem of Cade's polo shirt, pulling it over his head and instantly wishing there was more light in the room. For weeks he'd gotten the occasional glimpse of Cade's skin, and now he wanted to be able to look his fill. So he did the next best thing and let his fingers do the looking for him. Cade's belly was flat and smooth, his chest firm but not bulky. Cade groaned when Brian plucked at his small, perky nipples, and he figured to hell with seeing, listening was more than enough.

Brian let his hands wander along Cade's side, encountering a small scar that made him stop.

"I fell out of a tree," Cade whispered as he shivered. "It's still sensitive."

He hummed his agreement and continued his explorations, the smoothness of Cade's hips, the softness of the hair on Cade's legs. "Dang, you like that," Brian whispered into the darkness as Cade's breath hitched, and then Brian stroked behind his knee.

"It tickles."

Brian didn't want to tickle, so he trailed his hand up Cade's inner thigh until he reached the heat of his groin, opened his pants, and slowly tugged them off. Cade's breath hitched as Brian went slowly, committing each sensation to memory. When he cupped Cade's balls, he half hiccupped and half groaned. Brian wondered if he'd touched too hard, but Cade pressed upward, telling him it was okay.

"What do you want? You can have anything right now."

"Brian," Cade moaned wantonly, thrusting upward.

He kissed him, trailing his lips and tongue down the salty sweetness of Cade's neck to his musky, slightly sweaty chest. It had been a warm day, and that only seemed to bring out the intensity in Cade's skin. Hell, Brian's head spun, and he felt a little drunk. He felt better than drunk, because there would be no hangover or ill side effects, just Cade in his arms. Brian went on sucking a trail down Cade's stomach as muscles fluttered like bird wings under him.

When he reached Cade's cock, he licked the head before teasing his lips over it. Cade whimpered until Brian took mercy, sucking him a little deeper, the head of Cade's cock sliding along his tongue. Talk about intensity, Brian was well past drunk and approaching ecstatic. He sucked him deeper, listening as Cade's groan filled the small bedroom. Then he stilled, listening again.

"Brian," Cade whined, and he pulled away, kissing Cade with an intensity he never thought he'd feel as a clear-eyed realization thundered into him. Cade cared about him for him. It wasn't for the money or what he could get, but Cade cared for him. "What?"

"I think I finally get it." He sat back, looking at Cade's outline against the sheets. Now that his eyes had adjusted, he could see his chest and head, no detail but the basic form, perfect in the ways that mattered to him.

"What do you get?" Cade asked.

Brian wasn't sure he was ready to try to put it into words, but he shook at the idea that his entire life had been built on stupidity. "I'm just like my family."

Cade sat up, and his warm hands caressed Brian's cheeks. "You *were* like your family. You can be whoever you want to be." He leaned back, guiding Brian along with him. "Just let it go and be happy. That's all that really matters."

"But what if I mess up?"

"That's the thing about people who care for you—they will forgive instead of turning their back." Cade's voice was like a siren song.

Brian wanted to believe him, but his experience was so different. Still, Cade was here with him and had been when he needed him. Hell, Cade had put himself out for Brian, and no one had done that since his grandmother, and he knew she loved him. Brian asked himself if he loved Cade, making a leap from one idea to another.

"Stop thinking so hard and return to the present," Cade whispered into his ear before sucking on it. "Whatever questions you're wrestling with will still be there in the morning. Tonight, right now, you're mine, and I want all of you here with me, in the present."

Brian chuckled to himself. He had an amazing man in bed with him, and fuck all if he was going to let his family intrude on that, even in his thoughts. Brian pushed that aside and turned his attention back where it belonged. "Where was I?"

"I was hoping you were about to try to suck my brains out through my dick," Cade answered.

Brian nodded automatically. "Yeah. Now that sounds like a challenge." He kissed Cade one more time and then slid down his body, sliding his lips over Cade's semihardness, which firmed up instantly. Brian sucked him as hard and deeply as he could.

Cade came unglued under him, and damn if that wasn't the hottest thing he'd ever felt. Brian was a selfish lover, just like he had been with most everything else in his life. It was usually all about him, but with Cade, that didn't even cross his mind. It was all about Cade, the hitches in his breath, the shivers that ran though him like a tremor, the soft groans that grew in intensity and volume until a few times Brian thought Cade might have been trying to sing opera.

Brian knelt next to Cade, his cock sliding along his lips, tongue doing magical things, judging by the near shriek he pulled out of Cade. And when Cade's warm, firm fingers closed around Brian's cock, he nearly came right there. Brian was so keyed up by Cade's reactions that he'd forgotten about himself. He sucked harder, burying his nose in the soft hair at the base of Cade's dick and then slowly pulling away.

"I can't...." Cade's words shifted to babble before Cade tapped Brian on the shoulder. "Not like this."

Brian stopped dead still. "What?"

Cade yanked open a drawer near the bed and shoved a condom into Brian's hand, followed by what felt like a small bottle, probably lube.

Brian wasn't thinking particularly clearly, and instinct was taking over. "Are you sure? I...." He didn't wait for an answer. That took more time and care than he had in him right now. His only coherent thought was that he wouldn't hurt Cade, and from there, he dropped the condom on the bedding, sucking Cade to the hilt.

Cade went wild as Brian used all his oral skills to bring Cade all the pleasure he could. It didn't take long before Cade went wild under him, tensed, and released all his pent-up energy in a rush that hit the back of Brian's throat.

"Oh God, that...." Cade sighed as he lay still.

Now Brian could just see the contented lilt to Cade's lips and was supremely satisfied.

"You...."

"I'm glad you're happy," Brian whispered.

"Happy? You think you made me merely happy? That was awesome, stupendous, mind-blowing... and a whole lot of other things that I can't come up with right now because of the way you fried my brains." Cade was running a mile a minute once again.

"How do you do that? Everyone else would lay back unable to move after a big O like that, and you're like the Energizer Bunny."

Cade's energy level deflated instantly. "Is that bad?"

"God, no. It's just different, but not bad. Why? Did someone tell you it was bad?"

His anger was rising again, and it nearly bubbled over when Cade nodded.

"What kind of guys have you been dating?" Cade's energy was part of his charm. Nothing seemed to get him down, and he appreciated the good things in life like few people Brian had ever known.

"Just guys. One said I was weird because I didn't fall asleep the way he did after sex, and others seemed to agree."

Brian grabbed Cade, gently wrestling him down on the bed. Dang, he felt good against him, and when Brian's dick rubbed along Cade's hip, he nearly forgot what he wanted to say.

"That's a bunch of bull. I like your energy, and you should never hide it. I just remarked on it. I didn't want to make you feel bad." He had the ability to hurt Cade. That was eye opening. Others had hurt him, and he'd built walls to protect himself, but Cade didn't have those walls—either that or he'd allowed Brian around them.

"You're thinking again," Cade said playfully, grabbing Brian's butt and pressing against him. "That needs to stop for a while."

"But I think it's important," Brian said.

"More important than this?" Cade rolled them on the bed. "You were so good to me, and now it's my turn to return the favor in the best way I know how."

Brian was intrigued to say the least and lay back, watching as Cade straddled his legs, running his hands up and down Brian's chest and stomach in long, slow strokes. When he got close to Brian's dick, he raised his hips and held his breath, hoping Cade would touch him, but he stayed away.

"You're being mean," Brian groaned.

"Nope. You need to be patient." Cade leaned closer, his lips right near Brian's. "I should tell you that not all of the guys I was with were selfish and mean. My first lover wasn't. He was controlling and liked things his way. He also taught me that I was worth waiting for. I didn't learn that lesson at first, but I think I am now."

"Sweetheart, you are worth waiting a lifetime for." Brian was used to saying things like that to get what he wanted, but he meant it with Cade. He would wait for him.

"He also showed me that there is so much more to sex than just…." He grinned and reached between them, stroking Brian's dick.

"Okay," Brian agreed.

Cade leaned close to Brian's ear. "Men have lots of places that help turn them on, and I bet I know some of yours," Cade breathed, then licked along his earlobe.

Brian's eyes rolled to the back of his head, and he groaned long and low.

"See. I can feel your dick getting harder, throbbing between us."

"Yeah."

"There's also a place on your throat," Cade whispered as he licked down Brian's neck.

He lolled his head back, and sure enough, Cade zeroed in on a spot near his shoulder that sent heat running down his back.

"See, you can barely think now, and all you want is for me to take that long, thick cock of yours between my lips and suck you. When I do, you know you'll see stars, and that will be it."

"Jesus," Brian groaned. Where was this coming from, and what had happened to the Cade he thought he knew? But there was no way he was going to complain about finding out that Cade was a tiger in the bedroom.

"Yeah. Do I lie?"

"No?" Brian whimpered, unable to see straight.

"I can prove it."

Cade slowly slunk down him, his fingers trailing over skin that grew hotter and more sensitive wherever Cade touched. At times he could almost swear he was being burned, but there was no pain, only intensity that grew and compounded on itself.

Brian was ready to burst but determined to hold on for as long as possible. Heat raced through his veins, and when Cade reached his cock, he licked it, sending shudders through Brian. How could anyone do this to him? Cade had to have some special talent, some power over him, and if he did, Brian was more than willing to let him use it. When Cade opened his mouth and slowly sucked Brian's cock into it, Brian gripped the bedding, holding on for dear life. He didn't want to act like some teenager and come at the drop of a hat, but there was no way he could stop it. Cade took him deeper, and the tingling in his balls and at the base of his spine grew more and more intense, until Cade engulfed him and Brian lost the last of his control, tumbling into a mind-numbing release.

Brian was wiped out. He lay back, staring at the crack in the ceiling, exhausted, sated, and un-fucking-believably happy. Cade lay down next to him, and as Brian closed his eyes and tugged Cade into his arms, warmth spread through him, and Brian let contentment seep deep inside him.

"It was a great day," Cade said.

Brian kept his eyes closed. "Even with my family?"

Cade rolled a little closer. "They don't really matter. If you focus on what's important and ignore the rest, then the crap that doesn't matter won't have any bearing."

Brian wanted to believe him, and he so wanted his family to recede from his life, but nothing was that easy, not in his world. And the time he'd had with Cade had been a wonderful interlude, but he had the feeling that things were about to be shaken up again, especially with his appointment with the lawyer coming up soon.

CHAPTER 6

"So YOU got yourself a job," his grandfather said from the screen in the lawyer's conference room. "You worked for an entire month." In this recording he seemed visibly a little older than he had in the previous one. His eyes held a little less of their usual energy, and he breathed more heavily, as though he were out of breath. "Did you give Lydia an accounting of what you made and how much you had left?"

"Yes," Brian answered softly without thinking.

"Not much, was it? People work hard, and between taxes and the necessities of life, there isn't much left in the end. That's reality, Brian, and something you've been given. But make no mistake, I worked hard, very hard, when I was your age, and I saved my money so I could try to put it to work for me. I learned what I could from everyone around me, took it all in, and then used it to get what I wanted. But hard work was always in the mix. Never forget that if you work hard at whatever you do, success can follow. Without hard work, nothing ever comes to anyone."

The screen went blank, and Brian slowly turned his chair to face Lydia. Whatever his grandfather had in mind, he seemed to be leaving that up to her.

Brian knew his grandfather, but he was still trying to figure out the woman who sat across from him. "What's next?"

There was no file in front of her. It was just the two of them in the conference room. Her hands were folded, resting on the table.

"You were given two hundred and fifty dollars per week and told to get a job, which you seem to have done. Judging from the

uncashed checks in front of me, you managed to make it through."
Her expression showed that she'd had her doubts.

"I had some friends—well, a friend—who helped me," Brian
answered, growing wary. He'd managed to support himself and
had contributed to the rent.

Lydia slowly drummed her fingers on the table, saying
nothing. She seemed to be waiting.

"What do you want me to say?"

"It isn't me who's important. Say what you want to say."

"You mean like some grade-school report. What I did on my
summer vacation," Brian said as sarcastically as he could.

"What do you want to do with this?" she asked.

Brian shrugged.

"You do realize that these checks and the one you will receive
in a week represent almost a month of your work. Doesn't that
have any value to you?" She folded her hands once again.

"I don't know. I did what he asked," Brian said, motioning
toward the screen. "I learned that people have to work for money,
and I still have the job. Is that what he wants, for me to live on the
street? I'm staying with a friend, but I honestly don't know how
much longer I can do that."

"I'm well aware of where you're living and with whom. I
also know that you took him to your uncle's party a week or so ago
and that the family was less than impressed."

"So the fuck what?" Brian countered. "My family, the one
my grandfather built, is a steaming pile of crap. They're good for
nothing but looking out for themselves and wondering what they
can get from someone. All the people in my fucking life are. It
seems to be what they do."

"And you never saw that before? They haven't changed at
all. Your family is the same as they've always been. People act
according to their nature, and I'm afraid that's theirs. The more
important thing is, what is your character and nature?"

Brian didn't have a clue. His head ached, and he felt a little light-headed. His grandfather and Lydia, they wanted something from him, and it felt like he was in a test he hadn't studied for with a piece of paper covered in questions he didn't know any of the answers to.

Lydia slid the checks back across the table. "I want you to endorse them," she said.

Brian grabbed a pen from the holder in the center of the table. He scribbled his name on the back of both of them and stood up. "Are we done?" Anger welled. He hated being out of control and wanted to go home.

"Yes." She took the checks back and looked at them. "Other than what you want to do with these."

"I don't have a clue." He turned to the screen where his grandfather's face was frozen. "Maybe shove them up his ass. No, wait, he's fucking dead and still running my life. Everyone is always trying to do that." Brian walked around the table and yanked open the conference room door, then strode through the office until he reached the elevator.

Once the doors slid closed, he swore under his breath and slammed his fist into the wall. He wasn't sure why he'd gotten so angry. Yes, he was tired of this bullshit and just wanted to get to the end of it. More than once he'd wanted to call the whole sick thing off. Lydia had said he could go back to the way his life had been. His trust funds were still his, and he could flash his middle finger at his grandfather and everyone and be the person he'd been before, the one he understood.

The elevator doors slid open when he reached the ground floor. Brian didn't move right away, and they began to close once again. He'd thought about riding back up and trying to salvage what he'd ruined by storming out, but his pride wouldn't allow it. So he stopped the doors with his hand and stepped out, trying to decide what he should do next. He wanted to go home, so he left the building and used his new bus pass—he'd actually bought one—to ride back toward Cade's apartment.

It took him nearly the entire ride to realize that Cade's place was home to him. Cade was home. That sent a shiver running through him. Brian had no idea how much longer Cade was going to be willing to put up with him. At least Brian had spent the last week in Cade's bed with him instead of on the sofa. But Brian didn't fully understand what that meant. Did Cade really like him and care about him the way Brian hoped? He knew what sleeping with someone meant in his world. How fucking much could you get from them or what could they do for you. At least that seemed to be the attitude of the people who slept with Brian. Not that he'd known it at the time. He'd been completely oblivious then.

The bus stopped and went on. Brian got off at the stop closest to Cade's building and hurried toward it, walking faster the closer he got. He pulled open the front door and took the stairs two at a time. As he approached the apartment door, he heard Cade's voice from inside.

Cade was supposed to have been at work. Brian unlocked the door and opened it quietly. Cade was on the phone, and Brian didn't have to hear the specific words to recognize the distress in his voice.

"I understand, Mom, but there isn't anything I can do to help. You borrowed a couple hundred last week, and that took the last of my extra money." Cade ran his fingers through his hair. "What did you do with the rent money?" Cade paused. "That's good...." He waited once again. "And you're just telling me this now? Worry, of course I'll worry." Cade had his back to Brian and sank into a chair. "Okay. I'll see what I can do. I get paid in a few days, and I can send you something then."

Cade hung up, and Brian backed out of the apartment. Then he opened the door and pretended to have just arrived.

"How did it go?" Cade asked, and Brian saw him wipe his eyes before turning around.

He wanted to ask what was going on, but he'd walked into something that was none of his business, and Cade didn't seem to want to talk about it. "I don't know. I got mad and left. I'm getting tired of whatever game is being played with me."

Cade sighed so softly that Brian barely heard it.

"Not everyone is playing games with you. What if your grandfather really has a point to what he's doing and you're missing it? From what you've told me, he went through a great deal of time and effort to set all this up. Why not find out what's behind it?"

"He never cared about shit when he was alive. Why should he now that he's dead?"

Cade shook his head. "You don't know what your grandfather cared about. You're only assuming and projecting your hurt on him." Cade huffed and walked toward the short hallway to the bedroom. "People who care about you show it in different ways. If everything has to be your way, then you're going to be disappointed a lot."

Cade left the room, and Brian wondered if he should follow. The bedroom door closed more loudly than it usually did, and Brian wondered what he'd done wrong this time.

Brian couldn't take any more. He left the apartment, jogging down the stairs. He needed to take a walk and have a few minutes to think. When he left the building, he stopped and took a look in both directions, trying to figure out what he wanted to do. "Son of a bitch," he whispered under his breath and strode toward a black car parked halfway down the block. He hadn't thought about it until now, but Lydia was having him watched; she had to be. She'd known a lot about what he was doing, and now Brian had seen that same black BMW with the scratch on the trunk way too many times.

As he approached, he saw a man sitting in the front seat. Brian grinned and knocked on the window. "You need to do a better job of staying out of sight if you don't want me to see you."

One of the large men who had been outside his building turned to stare at him, saying nothing.

"I want you to find out what's going on with Cade's mother."

He shook his head, and Brian got a chill.

"You need to find things out for yourself."

Brian wanted to reach through the window and smack the bastard. The window rose, and the man pulled away from the curb and out into traffic. He watched him go and turned around. The anger that seemed to have settled over him since leaving the lawyer's had dissipated, and he wasn't in the mood for a walk any longer.

Brian had his ways of figuring things out, and they usually involved money and hiring someone. Now he couldn't do that, and asking Cade wasn't a possibility. He went back inside and quietly entered the apartment. Cade sat on the sofa in front of the television, but he didn't seem to be watching what was on. It was on the tip of his tongue to just ask Cade what was happening that had him so concerned, but he didn't know how to do it without seeming nosey, and Cade hadn't volunteered the information. Besides, he didn't want Cade to think he eavesdropped on his conversations, so he was stuck.

"You didn't take much of a walk," Cade observed.

"Sometimes the lawyer and this thing with my grandfather really fucking get to me. I keep wondering what he wants from me and why he didn't bother with me when he was alive."

Cade shrugged and turned away from the television. His eyes were a little puffy and filled with worry, and his lips were set with a touch of anger. Brian hoped that wasn't for him.

"You have to give people a chance. Sometimes they disappoint you in ways you never thought possible, and other times you never see the goodness coming."

That was how it had been with Cade. Brian always expected to be disappointed, so he never relied on anyone if he could help it. He'd been forced to rely on Cade, and he had been nothing but good to him and had shown him a kindness that Brian had honestly thought was long dead. "How can you be so upbeat all the time?"

"I'm not. I have plenty of shit in my life." Cade looked around. "Look at this place. I work two jobs and live in something so tiny that two people can't physically fit in the bathroom unless one of them is in the tub."

"I know why you do it," Brian said, thinking of Phillip. "If you had the chance, would you change anything?"

Cade hesitated as if thinking and then shook his head. "Would you?" Cade retorted, and Brian had to think about it before nodding.

The list of regrets and things he wished he'd done and could have had the chance to do was a long one.

"Then why don't you do them?"

"The people that I have the regrets about are dead. I can't change that." Brian walked to the sofa and sat down. "Fuck…. That's what my grandfather is trying to do, isn't it? He has or had his own regrets and is trying to change them or make up for them… or something."

"Maybe. Who knows?" Cade half shrugged again.

"Then how do I find out the answers?"

Cade's answer was fast. "By seeing whatever it is with this will through. My best guess is that it's the only way you are going to have a chance to get any of the answers you seem to want so badly."

"Then maybe I shouldn't have gotten pissed off at the lawyer," Brian commented.

Cade snickered. "If she's any good, she's used to it."

Brian wasn't so sure. Lydia didn't seem to be the kind of person to put up with much crap, but then she had been a friend of his grandfather's, so she had to be tough. His grandfather was never the easiest man to work for, but his people really seemed to love him. One thing was for sure, Brian didn't know as much as he should, and there was one person he knew could give him the information he wanted. Unfortunately that meant eating a healthy dose of crow.

He turned his attention to the television and let go of the worries for a little while. Eventually he moved closer to Cade and put an arm around his shoulder. Cade was tense and unusually quiet. Something was most definitely bothering him. Brian tried to catch his gaze, but Cade didn't seem to be particularly interested in any sort of communication.

"I need to get ready for work," Cade said after a while, and when Brian let him up, Cade disappeared into the bedroom and returned in his work uniform carrying a small bag. "I'll see you tonight. You might not want to wait up because you have to be at the club to open."

Brian stifled a groan and wondered if he still needed the job. After the first few weeks he'd gotten the hang of it and liked the people he worked with. They were nice enough and quite friendly. He'd seen a few of his former friends, but he paid them little mind now. They weren't worth the bother.

"I will," Brian said, knowing he wouldn't go to sleep until Cade came home.

Brian wasn't sure he was going to, but Cade gave him a quick kiss and then hurried out the door.

It took Brian about three minutes before he turned off the television and got ready to leave. He locked the door behind him and caught the bus on the corner, heading back downtown. If he was going to have to swallow his pride, he may as well get it over with.

"HOW CAN I help you?" the receptionist asked as he walked into Lydia's office.

He told her who he wanted to see and why.

"I'll see if she's in a meeting," she said, and Brian began pacing.

After a few minutes, he was ushered into the now-familiar conference room. Lydia came in a few minutes later and stood across from him, hands on the back of one of the chairs.

"I didn't expect to see you so soon," she said bluntly.

"I need some help. I know you've had me followed, so I suspect you know who I've been staying with and what he's done for me."

She had the grace not to deny it.

"So you know about Cade and his family."

She nodded after a few moments.

"Why?"

Lydia pointed to one of the chairs and pulled out the one she was holding, sitting slowly.

"One of your grandfather's hopes was that you would learn who your real friends were. I knew Marv from when he was first starting out. He gave me my first real start, and we were friends as well as associates. He held my daughter when she was born, and I was your mother's godmother. I bet you didn't know that."

Brian shook his head.

"I held you when you were a baby as well. Marv called and insisted I come over to see you. He was as proud as I ever saw him. Like I said, he and I were friends, real friends. He thought you had a bunch of hangers-on instead of real friends. That was why he wanted the money taken away. If any of your so-called friends stayed, then you would know they could be counted on."

"They deserted me like rats on a sinking ship."

"Exactly, and when Cade showed up, I had him looked into. His family is in need, and it's possible that he's hoping you'll come into money."

Brian shook his head. That was the last thing he thought about Cade. "He works two jobs so he can help his mother take care of his brother, Phillip. They're trying to save up so Phillip can move to a group home program and learn to be more independent."

"Brian…. There are no savings. Judging by what we can put together, everything they have is being used. Cade's mother is struggling each day to work and care for Phillip. There isn't anything left to save."

"But Cade…."

"Maybe he doesn't know," Lydia said and opened the folder she'd placed on the table earlier.

Brian saw his checks. "You asked me what I wanted to do with those."

She nodded.

"I want you to use it to find out what Phillip really needs and what's available for him."

She raised her eyebrows. "Are you sure?"

"Yes. I know it isn't much, but use what's there to pay someone to find out what options there are for Phillip."

She nodded. "I take it you've met him."

"Yes. Phillip is an innocent soul who adores Cade. He loves to color and has talent. He deserves a chance at the best life possible. I don't know what I can do to help, given my circumstances, but I can't do anything without knowing the facts."

"All right," Lydia agreed.

"Thank you." Brian got up to leave, and Lydia played his grandfather's video.

"So you've learned who your friends are," his grandfather said. "That's half the battle. After I made my money, I was shocked at the number of friends I had. Of course it was bullshit, and I always returned to the ones I'd known when I had nothing. They didn't want anything from me other than my friendship. Nothing else was required. If you've made a friend like that, just one, you are far better off than having dozens of the fair-weather people."

"I understand that now," Brian answered.

"Nurture those friendships. We all need people we can count on. The best friend I ever had was your grandmother. She was one of the few people who would tell me when I was full of shit. That's

110

invaluable. With money comes scores of people who want to tell you what you want to hear. That's meaningless. And I suppose in the process you've also learned that your family isn't among those friends."

Brian nodded.

"That's my fault, all of it. I gave them everything and made them work for nothing. I also spent my life in search of my dreams, but I gave little thought or paid little attention to the dreams of the others in my life."

Brian turned to Lydia and then back to the screen.

"Dreams are what make life interesting. So I want you to search for yours. What is it you want more than anything else in life?" The screen stilled.

"I can't have it," Brian answered instantly and turned to Lydia. "I know he's trying to somehow soothe his conscience or something, but what I really wanted, have always wanted, I can't have."

"Are you sure?"

"Yeah. I wanted his attention and my mother's so badly I could taste it. She went off to Africa to help others and left me at home. Starving kids were more important than I was to her. He—" Brian pointed at the stilled image. "He was always too busy being off on either a business trip or working to start a library, museum, or addition to the hospital to have time for me. I was less important to everyone in my life than their projects. The only one who gave a crap was my grandmother, and she left me too. So what I want, what I always wanted, isn't something I can have, so why dream about it?" His anger was rising again, but he held it in check. This was an old wound, and there was nothing he could do to change it. He'd tried when he was younger, asking to come along with them. All he'd wanted was to be near his mother and grandfather.

"Dreams are what power us to live," his grandfather said, and Brian turned toward the screen. "Never let anyone take those away from you, not me or anyone… ever."

"That's easy for you to say," Brian half screamed at the screen.

"I know I made mistakes, but as an adult, you need to make your own way in life. The past affects us, but we can either learn from it or let it rule our lives. My mistakes are my own, and I'll take responsibility for them, but you can't let them rule your life. So take off the shackles I saddled you with and let your heart soar."

The screen went blank, and Brian turned to Lydia.

"What does that mean?"

"He didn't share every detail with me. Some things he left up to interpretation. I'll get you a copy of the message so you can listen to it again, but if you want my advice, I think the answer needs to come from inside you."

"Great," Brian groaned. He stood, getting ready to leave. "What do I do now?"

She turned back to the screen. "Think about what it is that you truly want. Your grandfather always followed his dreams, and it led him to build everything your family has, but as he said in his own way, it came with a cost. So decide what your dream is, but don't ignore the price that dream will entail."

"All this seems like a lot of effort on his part…." Brian wasn't sure what his thoughts on the whole subject were at the moment, and he closed his mouth, not sure what he wanted to say.

"Yes. Your grandfather went to a lot of trouble." Lydia turned and put her hand on the door to open it.

"What if I'm not worth it?" Brian asked.

Lydia stopped, and when she turned around, she was smiling. Brian wondered what that meant.

"Like so many things in this world, in my experience, we have to make our own path, and examining our lives is a good thing. Only you can determine if what Marv went through was worth it, but just asking the question shows more depth and self-awareness than I think you had when I first met you a month or so ago." She let go of the doorknob and turned fully around. "Your grandfather saw something in you that he didn't in anyone else in the family, and I'm starting to understand what it is."

"Then tell me," Brian said.

"No. This is a journey you need to make for yourself. But I'd like to think you're on the right path." Lydia pulled open the door and left the conference room with Brian no more enlightened than he had been when he'd first arrived.

Brian took the bus back to Cade's apartment and spent the evening alone and restless. His grandfather had said that he wanted him to figure out what his dream was, but the things he'd always wished for, like to spend time with his mother and grandfather, were long past happening. They'd chosen their work over him, and maybe that was part of what his grandfather was trying to tell him. Except Brian didn't work, other than his job at the health club, and that wasn't an all-consuming passion the way their work had been for his grandfather and mother.

As time passed, Brian ran his grandfather's message around in his head. He got nowhere fast. When he heard Cade on the stairs, Brian realized he'd been sitting for hours without doing anything and began putting away the dishes he'd used for dinner.

"How was work?" Brian asked on this way to the kitchen.

"You should be in bed by now," Cade admonished as he dropped his bag near the door. "It was really busy, and they ran my legs off. We were short a server for a few hours, so I took over a few extra tables, and it was exhausting. I made really good tips, though."

Cade closed the door and shuffled off toward the back of the apartment, his shoulders sagging. Brian knew what Cade looked like when he was tired—he'd seen it often—but this was more than that.

Brian finished up in the kitchen and went down to the bedroom. He heard Cade inside, and when he came out, he shuffled to the bathroom in only his boxers, already half asleep by the looks of him. Brian waited until Cade was done and used the bathroom himself. Then he turned out the lights in the apartment and locked the door before joining Cade in the bedroom.

He was already asleep, judging by the even breathing and soft, warm snores that came from the far side of the bed. Brian was suddenly unsure of what Cade wanted. The last few nights Cade had always issued a specific invitation into his bed, but now there was only Cade's beautiful sleeping form.

Brian got undressed and placed his clothes over the wooden chair in the corner. Then he pulled back the light covers and got into bed. Cade rolled over and moved closer to him, his arm sliding across Brian's chest. He didn't speak and eventually rested his head on Brian's shoulder, using him as a pillow. Brian stared up at the ceiling, trying to will his mind to stop churning all the things over again and again. Of course he had zero success with that.

"You keep thinking too much," Cade eventually mumbled.

"I know, but I can't help it."

Cade didn't move. "Maybe that's because you keep trying to figure things out with your head when all you need to do is listen to your heart. The answers to the hard things are usually found there." Cade shifted a little, probably to get comfortable.

"How do you know?" Brian asked, but Cade's only answer was another of his soft snores, and Brian wondered if Cade had been talking in his sleep. He blinked his eyes a few times and figured he wasn't getting anywhere thinking about this all the time, so he closed his eyes and tried to let sleep take him.

CHAPTER 7

"I'M SUPPOSED to come up with a dream," Brian told Cade while they were at work the following day.

Cade checked an ID and scanned the member into the club. "That should be easy. What do you want most?"

"That's the problem. I don't know." Brian turned away and grabbed the bucket next to him so he could wipe down the various machines.

"Why not?"

"I feel like this is some sort of test. I don't even know why. But saying that my dream is to have my things and my life back isn't good enough. I think it's supposed to be bigger than that."

Cade paled slightly and turned away from him. The doors to the club opened, and a number of members filed in. Brian wanted to ask Cade about his reaction, but he was busy, and Brian figured he should get to work. He left the front desk and went into the workout room, then wiped down and dried the padded areas of each of the machines.

"Is this becoming a permanent thing with you?" Peter asked, and Brian instantly wished he'd looked around more closely.

He'd been doing his best to avoid his friend—or former friend. Hell, he had no idea who Peter was any longer. He did notice his expensive workout gear with the designer logo clearly visible and the way his pants were cut to show off his particular assets. He wanted to ask if Peter was there to work out or just to be seen. He rarely saw him actually using a machine. He was willing to bet that very few muscles actually got used, other than Peter's mouth, and not in a good way.

"I don't know," Brian answered honestly.

Peter turned toward the front lobby area. "I've seen you with the kid that works the front desk. He's cute and all, but I think you can do better."

"Excuse me?" Brian asked, wondering where this was coming from. "Cade is a great guy."

"Maybe he is, but the kid is probably only after your money. I mean, let's face it, whatever is going on with this will thing has to be temporary. You're Brian Paulson, and your family isn't going to leave you destitute. Maybe you did something to piss someone off, but you'll get back into their good graces, and the money will flow again." Peter glanced around like he was afraid he was going to be seen speaking with someone carrying a bucket and washed machines.

"Why are you talking to me, Peter?" Brian asked. "You haven't for the last few weeks. I've seen you walking the other way when I come near you." He stepped closer and lowered his voice. "I think it was you who was after the money, or if nothing else the fun it could buy. When I was in trouble I didn't see any offers of help coming from your direction. I've done a lot for you and with you over the years, but at the first sign of trouble, you were gone like a fart in the wind."

"Classy," Peter quipped with a roll of his eyes. "Did you pick that little saying up from your friend? Maybe you're better off like this." He leaned closer. "If I were you I'd do whatever it is that I had to in order to get my life back." He motioned in front of Brian. "This whole thing isn't a good look for you at all, and it certainly isn't helping with your reputation."

Brian dropped his cloth in the bucket, the water spattering and a few droplets flying toward Peter's shoes. Peter jumped back as though he might get burned.

"Sorry," Brian said with a small snicker. He was tiring of this conversation.

"You need to return to your own kind of people." He gaped down at the bucket of water. "Cleaning toilets just isn't your style."

With that last snide comment, Peter turned and stalked off. Brian started after him, wondering what had gotten into his now former—definitely former—friend.

"Brian," Cade said from behind him, and Brian bent down, picking the cloth out of the water. He wrung it out and went back to wiping down the machines. Cade stood next to him. "I think you need to find another place to live."

Brian's hand stilled midwipe. "Okay," he breathed, blinking and trying not to let the shock and disappointment show on his face.

"You can probably ask the lawyer to let you back in your place now. You did what your grandfather wanted and all."

Brian followed Cade's gaze to where he was watching Peter.

"Your friend is right. You don't belong here doing this. You have your whole life with all the money and privilege just waiting for you."

"You heard him?" Brian asked.

"Yeah. I got the gist of it. I'll give you a few days if you want to talk to the lawyer, but it's time we stopped playing house. Just tell the lawyer that your dream is to have your life back, and I bet she'll give it to you. Then you can quit working here and go back to your own life. That is your dream... right? That's what you said and what your friend seems to think."

"I don't know what my dream is. I told you that," Brian said, but the words sounded hollow to his own ears. The one thing he did know was that whatever his dream was, it had somehow involved Cade. But maybe he was mistaken about that as well.

"No. You said you thought this whole thing was a test and that you needed to come up with the answer. What if there isn't an answer other than being the person you are... or were?" Cade shrugged. "I need to go back to work." He walked away.

Brian shivered and wondered what in the hell he'd done. "Cade," he finally said, but if he was heard over the clang of machines and metal on metal, there was no indication.

"Is something wrong?" Garrett asked as he strode his way, and Brian shook his head, picking up the cloth again before going back to work. Thankfully Garrett seemed to have other things on his mind and didn't reprimand Brian.

As he worked, Brian churned the events of the last few days in his mind, and of course he came up with nothing. He knew he was missing something, but Brian would be damned if he understood what it was.

"YES?" LYDIA said and looked up from her desk when Brian barged in. He was still in his work outfit and carried the small bag with fresh clothes.

"I'm sorry," her assistant said as she followed Brian inside. "I did try to stop him."

Lydia lifted her hand slightly. "It's all right." She seemed completely unfazed by Brian's interruption. "What can I do for you?"

Brian slumped into one of the chairs. "I don't understand what's happening to me. Cade asked me to leave today because I told him about the whole dream thing, and I said that I didn't have one."

She folded her hands on the desk and seemed to be waiting him out. Finally she spoke. "I somehow think there's more to it than that." When Brian began to talk, she silenced him. "I'm not finished. If you wanted answers, I can't give you any. But if you want to begin to try to understand what's going on in your life, you need to look inward and not to others. I haven't changed, and neither has Cade. I'm willing to bet he's the same person he was when you met him."

"Then why is everything upside down and sideways?"

"Because you have changed, or I'd like to think you've changed and that you see things differently than you used to."

"But what do I do? I don't fit into Cade's life, or at least he doesn't think I do, and my friends… let me change that, the people I used to spend time with… they aren't what I thought they were."

Lydia laughed softly. "You have choices that most people could only dream of, and you don't know what to do with any of them. I think when your grandfather was asking you what your dream was, he wanted you to envision what the rest of your life would look like, and it was his way of telling you to decide your future and the kind of person you want to be."

"But how do I figure that out? I don't belong to either Cade's world or the one I came from."

"I have no answers to give you, but I can tell you this. Most of us live our lives in the world we were born in, and we never get a chance to see the other side. You have been given that gift. Maybe not in the way you wanted to get it…. And believe me, it is a gift. What you do with it is up to you." Lydia opened her desk drawer and pulled out a file that she passed across the desk. "Here is what you asked me to do for you." The file held only a few sheets of paper.

Brian thanked her and figured he was being dismissed, but he wasn't ready to leave yet. "What would you do if you were me?" he asked.

"I'm not you, and answering that question isn't fair to me or to you. See, your grandfather wasn't asking what my dream was. He already knew my dream and helped make it come true." She leaned forward slightly. "There weren't many women in my profession when I started out, and most of the women who graduated from law school were pigeonholed into family law. It was the way it was, but I wanted more. I worked hard, and when your grandfather called me because he needed some legal work done, I thought it was a crank call, and he thought I was the secretary. I will never forget asking, when he told me he needed someone tough to stand up for him in court, if he realized I was a woman." Lydia paused for a second with a wistful smile on her face. "He told me that he didn't care if his lawyer was a man or a dame, his words, as long as they had a spine of steel and were as hungry for success as he was. I'll have you know that your grandfather was the only man ever to call me that. Not even my husband dared to call me a dame. But he meant it in a way that was tough. To him dames were tough."

"I don't see how that helps," Brian said once he realized that was the end of the story.

"Then pull your head out of your butt."

That dame was out in force, Brian figured.

"Dreams come with a price, and my success nearly cost me my husband and family. It also changed my world. You say you don't think you fit into either your old world or Cade's world, and maybe that's true. But the only world that counts is Brian's world."

The light was starting to dawn; at least Brian hoped it was. "So you're saying I need to build my own world."

"And decide the kind of man you want to be," Lydia added as her phone rang softly and then silenced. "Now I have to get back to work, and you have some thinking to do."

She tapped the folder on the desk to draw his attention to it. At first Brian didn't understand why until she tapped it again. Then he knew she was quite possibly right. Whatever information was in that folder could prove to be the key to everything.

Brian picked up the file, stood, and then slowly sat back down as his curiosity got the better of him. Some of the information inside he already knew. The notes in the margin were enlightening to say the least. One said they needed to be careful of this guy, that he was after Brian for his money. That brought a smile to his face because Brian knew Cade wasn't like that. What startled him was the light the file shone on what Cade thought he knew. Cade had told Brian he was working hard so he and his mother could save up for Phillip to go to a special group home. But there was no money. Whatever Cade thought had been saved was gone, most likely spent by Cade's mother, who was more than a small financial mess. Heat and power disconnected multiple times, overdrafts, and more problems. How Lydia got this information he wasn't sure, but it was clear that Phillip wasn't going anywhere soon.

Brian turned the page and got another shock, but this one made him close the file, sit back, and think. While he waited, a plan began to come together, along with a picture of the life he wanted to lead.

Lydia clearing her throat pulled Brian out of his thoughts. She picked up the phone and said something quietly. While Brian watched, Emily came into the room carrying an old photo album. It was thin and had clearly seen better days. Lydia took it, thanked Emily, and then slid the album toward him. Brian sat still and didn't reach for it.

"This was among your grandfather's things, and I think it's something you should have. This isn't mentioned in the will, but I think you need to see what's in here."

Brian took the album and placed the now-closed folder on top of it.

"I WASN'T sure if you'd still be here when I got home," Cade said when he came inside.

He didn't look happy at all, and at first Brian wondered if Cade was pissed at him for still being here. He'd spent a lot of the rest of the day staring at the photo album on the coffee table. He found it made him angry, not because of what it held, but due to his own fear of opening the damn thing.

"You aren't going to get rid of me that easily." Brian rose and walked to where Cade stood in the doorway, drawn and exhausted. He took him by the hand and led Cade to the sofa. "Do you really want me to go?"

Cade's shoulders rose and fell. "You don't belong here. There's a whole life waiting for you, and all you have to do is snap your fingers and you can have it. Just ask the lawyer. This is only a game for you, but what little I have here is my life."

"I can see that. But it doesn't have to be. Any more than the life I had, the one that I drank myself through every day. I can choose the kind of life I want to lead, and I don't want to go back to what I had. My family pretty much sucks, and my friends were leeches. I see that now." He hopped on his knees on the sofa, bouncing a little as if he'd picked up some of the energy Cade usually had. "And I can change and build my own life."

"Congratulations on your enlightenment," Cade told him. "That's something that I'll never be able to do. I'm stuck in this apartment, and my family is never going to get out of the situation we're in. We were hoping to get Phillip into a group home, but the money we saved, that I thought we were saving, is gone. I know my mom spent it. So Phillip will stay where he is, and I'll continue working two jobs and my fingers to the bone until the day I die."

Cade knew. At least Brian didn't have to be the one to break that bad news to him.

"The thing is that the one person paying the biggest price in this whole mess is Phillip. He deserves a better life and a chance to learn to live on his own to a degree. And to be out from under my mother's ups and downs. She's a good person and really tries, but she can't manage money, and it slips through her fingers." Cade wiped his eyes with the back of his hand. "I can't do any more for her."

Brian pulled Cade into his arms and held him tightly. Until a month ago he hadn't had any idea what it was like to be without money, and he'd seen how hard Cade worked all the time. He was getting a clearer picture of Cade's life and his whole situation. It wasn't pretty.

"But if I don't help her, then Phillip is the one who suffers, and I can't let that happen." Cade began to shake.

"Did she lose her job?" Brian asked.

"No. But she went to the casino with friends after work and lost some money that she couldn't afford to lose. So she didn't have the money for the utilities. What I don't know is where Phillip was when she was doing this. Probably with the caretaker. At least she's paid by the county and state directly, so my mother can't get her hands on that money." Cade took a deep breath and released it haltingly, lifting his head so Brian could see his face. "I'm sorry I overreacted at the club today. I saw you with that Peter guy and kept thinking I could never compete with him. He has everything, and I have nothing."

"You don't have to compete with Peter or anyone else." Brian closed the distance between them, kissing Cade with as much gentleness and care as he could muster. Brian hadn't been going for massive heat, but it bloomed between them nonetheless. Brian was finding that having Cade in his arms was where he wanted to be. "He has nothing on you. Never did."

"But...," Cade began.

"Peter is a jerk who only wanted me for what I could give him and nothing more. He may have been my friend once, but that's over. I don't need people like him in my life." What he needed was the man he held in his arms at that very moment.

Sometimes things happen in a flash of enlightenment, and other times lessons have to be learned slowly. Brian realized he'd had some of both. The realization of what he wanted had been building for a while, but it wasn't until that kiss and the threat of losing what he wanted that everything came into focus. "I still don't have a dream like my grandfather says I should." He kept coming back to that, and his head wouldn't let him move too far away from it for some reason.

"Yes, you do," Cade said. "You told me once that the people who were most important to you always put you second behind their projects, and you wished you could change that."

"Yeah. That's true. But all the money in the world isn't going to let me go back in time."

123

"Duh," Cade said as he tapped Brian on the head. "You're missing the point. You want people in your life who will put you first. It's that simple, a family of your own."

Cade blinked at him for a few seconds, and Brian knew he was right. That was all he really wanted. What shocked him was that he didn't care if they were rich or poor, only that they were his... that Cade was his. Brian tugged him closer once again, kissing him deeply.

"I think it's time we got you in bed. I have to work in the morning."

"And I have to work at the restaurant," Cade groaned.

Brian could see where holding down both jobs was wearing Cade out. Brian stood slowly and tugged Cade to his feet. He shooed him down the hall to clean up while Brian locked the door and turned out the lights. Brian heard water running and turned down the covers, got undressed and into bed.

When Cade stepped into the room, Brian's mouth went dry. Cade was gorgeous and made Brian ache for him. His cock throbbed, bouncing the sheet over him.

"Man, I think it's been too long," Cade said with a grin, noticing Brian's reaction.

"It has," Brian breathed and lifted the covers, tugging Cade to him as soon as he was close enough. Finally Brian understood what was important in his life. "But it's always too long when it comes to you. We were together just a few days ago, and it seems like a lifetime." Brian sucked at one of Cade's nipples, and he groaned softly, sending a wave of need running through him. "Damn."

"What?"

"The sounds you make for me."

Brian smiled and went back to his ministrations, seeing how many different tones he could get. That special place on the side of Cade's hip earned a deep, throaty moan, while a swirl of his tongue in Cade's belly button earned a sharp, high whimper that went on as Brian licked his way lower and lower, encircling the head of Cade's cock with his lips and then taking him deeper.

He slowly worked his mouth lower, hearing the groans turning to pants and then a long, satisfying sigh. Brian added his own as Cade's rich, salty, and slightly sweet flavor burst on his tongue. Damn, he loved being with Cade, tasting Cade, running his hands up and down his chest and belly as Cade pressed forward to his touch. What was most amazing was that Cade seemed to need him as much as Brian needed Cade. He was drawn to Cade's attraction, and it created an unending circle of desire that Brian was more than happy to feed on.

"Brian," Cade whispered breathlessly and held Brian's head. "You're going to pull me over, and that will be the end."

He let Cade slip from between his lips and climbed up him, never breaking eye contact. When they kissed, Cade hummed softly and wrapped his arms around Brian's neck, holding them close together and chest to chest. Brian ground his hips slightly, just enough to send a ping of sensation through both of them. God, that felt good. Cade's skin was silky, and there was just enough slick between them to smooth the way.

Cade wrapped his legs around Brian's waist and stretched, reaching to the nightstand. Brian leaned over and managed to pull the drawer open without spilling the contents. He grabbed a condom and located the bottle that had rolled inside before returning his attention to Cade.

Brian's heart raced, and his skin heated at the thought of being inside Cade. He managed to roll on the condom with his shaky hands and didn't spill the lube all over the bed. Once he was ready and after he'd spent time preparing Cade—God, he loved everything about him—Brian pressed to Cade's tight little entrance and slowly rocked his way inside. Cade gasped, and Brian stopped, holding still while the pressure and heat pulled him in. He had to wait until Cade was ready, no matter what his instinct told him to do. Ignoring his own needs and the call of his body was hard, but he held still until Cade tapped his hip. Then he pressed deeper, letting Cade's body surround him.

Brian had had sex many times, and he knew what it felt like to be surrounded by someone else, but this was different, hotter and so much more intense. He knew it wasn't because of a different physical reaction on his part but Cade's reaction to him. Brian's hearing, sight, and touch were on overdrive. Every sensation, each sound and tingle, was new and exciting. Small moans may as well have been loud cries of passion, because that was how they sounded to Brian, and Cade's gentle touches were like they'd been heated in a blast furnace. Brian wanted this to go on forever.

Their sloppy kisses and the way Cade clutched him was hot enough, but the look in Cade's eyes, the swirls of blue, the small gasps for breath, all added to the intensity. With each thrust, every movement, all of Brian's energy was taken, magnified, and sent back to him. It left Brian nearly unable to pull air into his lungs, and little points of light formed around the edges of his sight. He wasn't going to stop and inhaled deeply while he continued making love to Cade. He wanted to be with him like this forever, hold him and protect him from everything bad. Cade deserved only the best love and care possible, and in the course of making love, Brian was determined that he should have them.

"Damn, I don't know how I lived before I met you," Brian gritted between his teeth as pressure built inside him. He stared deeply into Cade's eyes.

"You were you," Cade told him and gasped, arching his back. "You're still you… only better… I hope."

Brian would have wondered if Cade was correct, but he was too overwhelmed with lust to let Cade's words sink in. Brian was used to saying what he needed to in order to get the things he wanted or people to do what he wanted. But what he said to Cade had meaning, and it had to be right. "You feel so right." He was probably rambling a little, but extreme desire had loosened his words. "And I don't want to let you go."

Cade groaned, and Brian felt his hand sliding back and forth between them as he leaned forward to capture Cade's sweet lips. He loved kissing him almost as much as he adored the sensation of being surrounded by him. Cade was amazing, magnificent, and Brian knew he had truly been given a gift the day he tripped that mugger in the park. Brian had flashes of his life without Cade and realized how empty it had been. He knew this was a weird time for these realizations, and they flitted away as pressure and passion built until Cade's amazing eyes and the grip of his body were all he could think of. The rest could wait until later.

"Cade," Brian groaned. "You make me feel special."

"You are special," Cade answered, and those words sent him racing over the edge of delicious oblivion.

Through his haze of release, he felt Cade clench around him, adding to the euphoria as Brian realized Cade was following him into release.

Brian held Cade as he lay quietly, his soft breath tickling Brian's ear. He was growing to love everything about this man, and letting him go wasn't something he wanted to happen.

"What are you worrying about now?" Cade asked. "I can hear the gears turning."

"I…." Brian pushed himself upward so he could look into Cade's eyes once more. "What if I'm not good enough for you?"

"Is that what's really gotten into your head?" Cade asked, smoothing the hair from Brian's forehead.

"Yeah. I wasn't good enough for the rest of my family… my mother… or my grandfather… so why should I be good enough for you? You're better than all of them."

"How do you know that?"

"Because of the way you look at me," Brian whispered.

"How do I look at you?" Cade tilted his head slightly.

"Like I'm someone special." Brian met Cade's intense gaze. "Maybe like I'm the most important person. That was all I ever wanted."

Just like that, Brian knew that in a way, his dream, the one he'd had for so many years, had come true. Cade smiled and pulled him down into a searing kiss that left Brian wondering if Cade was trying to start a fire for round two.

However a few minutes later Cade yawned, and Brian got out of bed, grabbed a cloth from the bathroom, and cleaned them both up before rejoining Cade under the covers. The night was cool, and Cade rolled over, pressing close to him. Brian held him and lay on his back, staring up at the ceiling. Could it be that simple? Brian wasn't sure, but after work the following day, he had to find out.

BRIAN GOT up early the following morning. He couldn't sleep, and even though he was supposed to be at work when the club opened, it was still too early to leave. Thankfully, Cade was off at the club today and could sleep in. He needed it. He hadn't even moved when Brian got out of the bed and went into the living room.

Brian sat on the sofa, staring at that damned album once again. He wasn't sure exactly what he was afraid of. He reached for it, set it on his lap, and opened the first page. Brian had expected one of those old photo albums with the semisticky pages with sheets of plastic that went over the pictures. This was a scrapbook of sorts, and the picture of a smiling toddler stared out at him. He recognized his own, much younger, image. Brian turned another page, and there were pictures of him with his grandfather, then his mother. He figured his grandmother had put this together, and when he turned the page again, Brian smiled at the image of him standing on the chair in the kitchen, an apron on and a huge wooden spoon in his hand, with his grandmother next to him. Brian closed his eyes as memories of the time they spent together, baking in that huge kitchen, washed over him.

It was almost enough for him to close the album, but he blinked away the tears that threatened to pool in his eyes and kept going, the page making a crinkling sound when he moved it. There were pictures of him on a pony, Grandpa leading him around. Some of him swimming in the pool, his mother holding him, grinning. God, he missed her. The tears welled, and this time Brian didn't try to stop them. He expected anger, but none came. All that Brian got was the sadness and loss that he'd tried to bottle up for all those years. He continued turning the pages of pictures of his childhood. When he got to one of his mother alone in what looked like an office in a tent of some kind, Brian snapped the book shut.

"What's wrong?" Cade asked, and Brian turned around to where he stood naked at the door. Cade walked to where Brian sat, flopped down next to him, and pulled the light blanket from the back of the sofa over himself.

"Nothing," Brian lied. "Lydia gave me this yesterday."

Cade reached for it and opened it once again. The book came open to the picture he'd seen last. "Is this your mom? She was pretty." Cade continued looking. "Was this taken when she was at work?"

"Yeah. From the look of it, not too long before she died." Brian sniffed. "I remember writing her a letter asking if she'd let me come visit her there. I wanted to be with her."

"What did she say?" Cade asked.

Brian shook his head, unable to speak at first. "I never got an answer."

Cade continued looking at the photo, then placed the album back on Brian's lap. "What's that?" Cade asked.

Brian leaned in closer to look. The picture was grainy, like someone had had the original enlarged. "Papers...," Brian began. "No. Those are drawings." He turned to Cade, blinking once again. "Those are my drawings. I sent them to her along with the letter." They were right behind her, close to her in a way Brian couldn't have been. "I don't want to see any more."

He went to close the album, but Cade stopped him and opened it again, turning the page.

A letter was affixed to the next page, with the others empty. Unlike the other pages, which had been embellished with brightly colored paper, this page was only the letter. Brian stared at it. The letter was addressed to him in his mother's flowing handwriting. She may have been a doctor, but she never had the handwriting of one.

> *Dear Brian, my darling boy,*
> *I miss you more than I can possibly tell you.*
> *I got your letter, and I'm afraid you can't come*
> *see me. It's too dangerous, but we're making real*
> *headway on this disease. The hospital is set up, and*
> *it's beginning to run well, so I'm planning to come*
> *home in the next few weeks, and this time I promise*
> *I'll stay for good. I did what I really wanted to be*
> *able to do and set up my own hospital from the*
> *ground up, the way I always wanted. The people*
> *here will benefit from my work for years to come.*
> *And that's good. But now it's time I was home with*
> *you and your father. I want you to know that I miss*
> *you and that you are always with me no matter what*
> *I do or where I go.*
> *I promise I won't be going anywhere again. I'm*
> *looking forward to your hugs and some more of your*
> *amazing pictures. I put the ones you sent in my office*
> *here. Start making a list of the things you want to do*
> *when I get there.*
> *I love you more than anything,*
> *Mom*

Brian closed the album and stared blankly at the wall as many of the assumptions he'd built up in his mind over the last decade and a half came crashing down around him. His mother had loved him, and she had been coming home to be with him.

In the end she had said in a way that he was more important than her work. Brian turned to Cade and leaned his head against his shoulder, letting go of some of the pain he'd carried around for so long.

CHAPTER 8

"I DON'T think I have a dream like the one my grandfather wants or thought I should have," Brian said the following afternoon as he sat across from Lydia and Emily. "See, my dream was to have my grandfather and mother put me first and spend time with me. But they were always off doing something they felt more important."

Lydia nodded.

"But I now think they were out pursuing some part of their dreams. I'd like to think that my mother was a good doctor, so maybe helping people was what she wanted to do." Brian swallowed hard and sighed. "I wish they had thought enough to let me be part of their dreams rather than left on the outside, looking in."

Lydia nodded but said nothing.

"So that's my answer. I already had my dream come true because I found Cade, and I never would have if it hadn't been for this whole will thing, weird as that may sound. But I'm going to try to build a life with Cade, and I'm going to try to put him first in my life. I think the thing I learned most from this is what's truly important."

Lydia turned to Emily and then back to him. "Is that all you have to say? I know that was what you always wanted, but I think I'd like to hear your dream for the future. What is it you want most when you close your eyes? Your grandfather believed in trying to make the world better. He didn't just live for himself, even though you may think so. Your mother didn't either."

"I see that now. It doesn't change how I feel, but it does help me understand why they acted the way they did. It doesn't mean

I'm happy about it. But what's done is done, and I can either let that anger run my life or I can let it go. So the final point is that I don't know what I see for my future, and I don't have some grand dream or cause for it. Right now I want to be able to live my life and be happy with it. I like to think I've made a start on that, but only time will tell." Brian stood up to leave. "I know that isn't the answer my grandfather wanted, but it's the best one I have." He was at peace in a way.

The letter from his mother had said she'd been doing something she loved and that she had really accomplished something. Brian assumed that setting up the hospital had been her dream, and he couldn't blame her for wanting to fulfill it. That she'd accomplished it and was coming home when she'd gotten ill was a consolation. Her dream had still cost him his mother, but he could understand her better now, and he was less angry about it.

"Thank you for everything and for giving me the album," Brian said to Lydia. "It helped me a great deal." He backed away from the chair. "Whatever has been going on with Grandpa's will is over. I know I haven't fulfilled whatever he wanted, and you know, that's okay." He pulled open the conference room door.

"Brian," Lydia said. When he turned around, she pointed toward the chair. "I think you underestimate yourself and your grandfather. You did have a dream, and somehow you managed to fulfill it."

"Yes." In a way he had. He'd wanted things to be different between him and his mother. That was foremost, and he'd gotten that. Just knowing he was important to her and that she was coming home to him and his dad was enough to soothe a wound that had never truly healed.

Lydia opened the file that seemed almost ever-present at these meetings and pulled out an envelope. "This is earmarked for you at this time."

She passed it over to him, and Brian opened the envelope and stared at a check for fifty million dollars.

"That is for you to do with any way you please. Also, your car is out front, your funds have been released, and you are free to return to the condo."

Brian nodded, barely hearing her words as he stared at the check. "That's it?" he asked. It seemed rather anticlimactic to be holding only a check. After everything, he was left with a simple check. Granted, it was a large one, but…. He had expected to be happy when he came to the end of all this, and he was, but he was also a little sad as well. "Don't think me ungrateful, but I guess I thought I'd feel differently when I got to this point."

"What did you expect to feel?" Lydia asked.

"I don't know. I expected to be happy, but this check… it represents another set of changes." It was a key for him to go back to the life he'd had and enough money of his own that he could stay away from his family and be independent. He could have the life he'd always wanted without a care in the world.

"Change in itself is often neither good nor bad. It's what we do with the opportunities that come with change that counts."

"Where did you hear that from?" Brian asked with amusement.

"Your grandfather. It was one of the things he said whenever the team would get upset or nervous about something. Right after that, Marv usually thought briefly, made a decision, and went full steam ahead without ever looking back." Lydia walked around the table. "I know this put you through some hardships and was more than a little inconvenient, but your grandfather wanted you to learn some things and to try to keep you from making the same mistakes he did. Only you can decide if he succeeded or not, but the changes I see in you make me proud, and I know they would make your grandfather feel the same way."

Brian shook her hand and nodded with a small smile. "Thank you."

"I'm always here if you need anything, including financial advice." She chuckled. "I'm happy it turned out this way."

She pulled open the door, and Brian stepped out of the office and rode down to the ground floor in the elevator. When he left the building, his car was parked right in front, and one of the huge guys who'd kept him out of his condo handed him the keys. Brian took them and slid into the leather seat, pulling the door closed and grinning as he looked out the front window. He blew air from between his lips and started the engine, listening to it purr. Then he pulled out and into traffic.

It took him only a few blocks before he realized he didn't know exactly where he was going. He continued straight for another block and made the left turn to head out toward Cade's building until he remembered that Cade wasn't home. Still, he continued on and parked out front, then hurried up the stairs and inside that apartment, hearing the house phone ringing as he unlocked the door.

"Hello," he said breathlessly on what he was certain was the final ring.

"Oh, thank God, you're home," he heard Cade's mother say in a near panic. "Brian, I got called to an appointment with Phillip's social worker. They said there may be a place for him at a school that can work with him. I need to go and check it out, but I have to be there in an hour. Cade's at work and…." She sounded on the verge of a breakdown.

"It's all right. I just got home, so if you need someone to watch Phillip, bring him over."

"Oh, goodness. Thank you." She sounded like the weight of the world had just lifted off her shoulders. "We'll be leaving in a few minutes."

The call disconnected, and Brian wondered if he should let Cade know what was going on, but the restaurant frowned on calls, so he texted him and went in search of the things Cade kept for when his brother visited.

Fifteen minutes later he heard footsteps on the stairs. Phillip burst in with a huge smile. Brian always loved how this grown-man-sized person smiled with the joy of a child.

"I set out coloring books and crayons for you, and we can watch cartoons if you want to."

Phillip engulfed Brian in a hug, and his mother walked tiredly inside.

"You're like my second brother," Phillip said, and Brian wasn't sure what to say to that.

He lightly patted Phillip on the back and met Shirley's drawn eyes.

"I don't know how long I'll be," she said softly.

"It's all right. There is plenty to eat, and if Phillip wants, we can order a pizza or something."

"With sausage and pepperonis?" Phillip asked, and Brian had his answer. Pizza it was.

"We'll be fine."

He said good-bye, and Shirley hurried out to her meeting.

"What shall we do first?"

Phillip pulled out one of the kitchen chairs and set to coloring happily. Cade called a few minutes after his mother left.

"Is everything okay? I only have a few minutes to talk."

"It's fine. Phillip and I are here, and we're going to order pizza for dinner. Don't worry about anything."

"How long did she say she'd be?" Cade asked.

"I don't know, but we'll be just fine together." Brian smiled as they ended the call.

A few hours later he ordered a pizza and had it delivered. He'd have been lying if he hadn't wondered what was happening as the hours went on with no additional call or word from Shirley. At almost ten, Cade hurried in.

"They let me off work early," he said, out of breath. "She still isn't back?"

"No," Brian said softly. Phillip had curled up on the sofa to watch television and had fallen asleep about an hour earlier. "She looked haggard and really tired when she was here. I don't know if there's something wrong with her, but she didn't look well."

Cade tried calling and didn't receive an answer. He hung up and put his phone on the coffee table. "Did you meet with the lawyer today? I saw your car outside, so something happened."

Brian nodded.

"Did it go okay?" Cade asked, and Brian reached into his pocket. He pulled out the check and handed it to Cade, who opened it and gasped. "They gave you this?"

"Yeah. They also restored access to my trust money, and I can return to the condo."

"So you have everything you wanted." Cade turned away and checked on Phillip. "When will you go home?" Cade asked, and it was like a punch to the gut.

Over the past few weeks he had really begun to think of this small apartment and its single occupant as home.

"I have things well in hand here. I'm sure my mom will be back at any time, and if Phillip has to stay the night, then I can call into work in the morning to take care of him." Cade straightened up, but he didn't turn around. "Will you give Garrett your notice? I can't see you continuing to work now that you have all that."

"Cade… I…."

"You don't have to say anything else. I know you don't intend to continue to live this kind of life. Why would you? I know I wouldn't." Cade finally turned around.

"This is stupid," Brian said, holding out the check.

"What are you doing?" Cade gasped.

"Making you understand. This is only a check. It's only money. I'll rip the damned thing up and go without it if that's what you want." Brian stared at Cade, ready at the slightest nod to tear up the check. He knew of course that getting another would be easy, but this was symbolic. He wasn't going to be without Cade. "You are more important than the money."

"Brian," Cade said as he walked over and lightly touched his hands.

Brian released one side of the check and put it back in his pocket.

"Are you crazy?"

"No. I'm definitely not. And I know what I want. This whole process has taught me what's important." He tugged Cade into the bedroom and closed the door. "I want the people in my life to be what's truly important, not the damned money. And I want you. The man who took me off the street and helped me when I was damned near humiliated and had nowhere to go. You didn't have to do any of that at all, but you did."

"Are you sure? I'm just a guy who was nice to you. I don't fit in the world of your family."

"You certainly charmed a lot of the people at the party." Brian wished he hadn't said those words as soon as they crossed his lips.

"See? That's still what's important to you. The money is back, so you'll return to your life, and you want me in tow. But I can't do that. I don't want to be part of those people. Most of them were fake, and being with them is going to make me just as fake."

Brian shook his head hard. "I don't want to return to that either. I want to build my own life with the people who care about me and those I care for. And it all starts with you. Don't you see that? You make me want to be a better person." Brian paused at the hardness in Cade's eyes. "Words aren't going to be enough," he said out loud. "Then I'll show you the kind of person I am." Brian backed away. "I promise you."

"How do you plan to do that?" Cade asked skeptically.

"I don't know. But it's important that I do. You're important." He turned to leave the room.

"I don't understand why a guy like you with the world at his feet would want someone like me. I know you've stayed here and we've been together and all, but…."

"Did you really think I was with you because I wanted a place to live or that I was just with you for a good time?" That notion hurt, but he tamped it down.

Cade swallowed and finally shook his head.

"Then why say it?"

"Maybe because I just find it hard to believe. There are so many other guys who would be so much better for you than I can be." He turned toward the door. "Look at my family… look at me. You'll be wearing your designer clothes and everything that money can buy." He shook his head. "Remember, I'm the guy who taught you how to shop at Goodwill."

Brian sighed loudly. "I remember that. But I also remember that you were the one who was there for me, the only one, and I have to tell you that I'm not the same self-obsessed guy that you invited to stay with you a month ago. Or at least I hope I'm not."

Cade blinked a few times. "So you're serious about wanting to be with me?"

"Yes. But I have to make sure you don't have any doubt. Hell, I have to know that I don't have doubts—not about you, but about myself. There have been a lot of eye-opening experiences in the last few weeks, and I can't expect you to believe that I've changed so much." Brian reached for the bedroom door and pulled it open, then stepped out into the living room.

"Are you leaving?" Cade asked.

"Not until we hear something from your mother." He crossed his arms over his chest and settled into one of Cade's chairs. What he needed was an idea for what he could do to show Cade how much he cared. Before, the old Brian would have gone to a jewelry store and bought Cade something shiny and expensive, maybe a gold watch. But that wasn't the kind of thing he wanted. It had to mean more than that, whatever he did. It had to demonstrate to

Cade how much he meant and that Brian didn't see the world the same way he had.

Brian ended up sitting quietly in the chair, thinking and watching Phillip sleep. Cade sat in the other chair, his head soon bobbing back as fatigue caught up with him. As Cade fell asleep, Phillip startled awake, sitting up and rubbing his eyes. Brian put his finger to his lips, and Phillip nodded, getting up and walking quietly to the bathroom. When he returned, Phillip went to the table to color once again, and Brian joined him, looking over at Cade.

"He's asleep," Phillip whispered. "Where's Mama?"

"We're waiting for her to come back."

Brian didn't want him to worry, even though his own concern was increasing with each passing second. Phillip went back to coloring without a care as Brian turned on a small kitchen light.

"Mama said she'd be back," Phillip told him. "Mama always does what she says."

Brian was beginning to wonder if that was true, but he didn't argue. He checked the clock on the stove, and it showed that it was approaching eleven. "Do you want a snack?"

Phillip nodded, and Brian got up to get him something.

"I want to go home to bed. I'm tired."

"I know." Brian turned to the door for the millionth time, willing Shirley to come through it. He returned to the table with some cheese and crackers on a plate, and Phillip took some, eating the cheese between crackers like a sandwich. Once he'd had one, he returned to his picture of flowers, tongue between his teeth as he concentrated.

"Phillip, if you could have anything in the world, what would it be?" Brian asked. He'd had so many questions about dreams, and he was curious what Phillips's were.

"I want a new bicycle." Phillip didn't stop coloring. "And maybe I'd like to go to a school like Mama told me about, where I could be with other guys like me." Phillip put down his colored pencil. "I know I'm different," he said haltingly. "I need special help because I don't learn new things fast."

Brian had no idea what to say to that. He decided to be honest. "Everyone learns new things at different speeds."

Phillip put down his pencil. "I'm not blind. I see how people look at me sometimes." He shrugged. "Mama says it's because I'm special."

"Your mama's right," Brian told him right away. "So you want to go to school?"

Phillip nodded. "I want to be able to take care of myself, and I want to maybe fall in love with someone and be happy like they do in the movies. I want to make sandwiches and go to the grocery store. Mama says that they will teach me how to have my own money and everything." He smiled brightly and then grew serious and leaned over the table. "Mama doesn't think I know things, but I do. I heard her on the phone, and she said that I can't go there."

"What did Mama actually say?" Cade asked before yawning, and Phillip closed his mouth tight.

It was almost cute. Brian expected him to lock his lips and throw away the key.

"I'm not mad at you or Mama. I promise."

Phillip stood up and walked to Cade, hugged him and received one in turn from his brother. "She was on the phone to someone, and she said that this school was already full."

Cade turned white, and then just as quickly color rose in his cheeks. Brian had to keep his attention on Phillip in order to try not to upset him.

"It's all right. There will be other schools and places that you'll be able to go and learn," Cade said.

Phillip backed away from Cade, looking up at him, and thankfully Cade managed to school his surprise.

"Why don't you go lie down again, and we'll wake you when Mama gets here," Cade told his brother gently, and Phillip lay down on the sofa, curling under the blankets.

Brian went into the kitchen and dimmed the light.

"What do you mean, and how did you find out?"

"As part of this whole thing with my grandfather's will, Lydia investigated you and your family. She gave me a copy of the file. The thing is that there is no money for his schooling. There may be a special private school for him, but any money for it is gone. Your mother spent any of the money that you were sending for him." He kept his voice as low as he could.

"And you knew…."

"I saw what was in the file, at least some of it, but I thought I should… I don't know, try to forget that I'd seen it? I wanted to try to figure out a way to help, and when I saw the information, I realized that what I'd done was pry into your family's private life." He knew he sounded lame, but it was the truth.

"So you said nothing."

"It wasn't my information to tell. What was I supposed to do? Blurt out that your mother had been lying to you? I was hoping to make things right for him, but I didn't know how."

Cade touched Brian's chest over his pocket. "And now that you've got all this, you're going to what…? Throw some money at the problem? I don't think so."

Cade was furious, judging by the way his eyes bugged and his words hissed from between his teeth. Brian hoped the worst of his anger was directed at his mother.

"I didn't have anything at that time, but I would like to help Phillip, and you, if you'd let me."

"So you'd pay for his schooling? See, I did my research too, and the school that would be the best fit for him is in Madison, over an hour away. It's run as part of the university there, and it's an amazing program. But how is Phillip going to feel if he's there and I have to be here to work? I'll only get to see him when I can afford to take the bus over. I don't have a car. And for the record, I'm not going to have you paying for his school. I'll figure out something myself, even if it means getting a third job."

That wasn't what Brian had envisioned at all. Phillip needed to stay near his family, near Cade. "I don't want Phillip to go to Madison either." He should have done his own research rather than asking someone else to do it for him. If he had, he might have known that particular fact. "Being with his family is important." Brian turned to Phillip, who was asleep once again. "What do we do? It's what he wants."

"I know," Cade whispered and moved into Brian's arms. "I can't take your money to pay for it."

"Aren't there programs here in town?"

"There are, but they aren't as good as the one there. There, the people live in small groups and learn together how to cope with some of the challenges of life. Some will never be fully independent, but they are taught to do the most that they can for themselves. Here, the programs are run by Social Services, and that means they are subject to budget cuts and restrictions. You know how things are."

"I do." Brian put his arms around Cade. Now that the storm had passed, Cade's exhaustion seemed to be catching up with him.

Footsteps on the stairs followed by a soft knock announced Shirley's return.

"I got called into work right after my meeting with the school."

"You didn't go all the way to Madison, did you?" Cade asked skeptically.

His mother shook her head. "I was meeting with one of the social workers who can get Phillip into a program here. It isn't as good, but it's the best we can do."

She looked even more tired than she'd been earlier, and older. It was obvious to Brian that she was having a hard time keeping all of the parts of her life in balance. Shirley hurried over to Phillip, who was still sound asleep, and then returned to them.

"Thank you for watching him."

"Mom, I thought we were saving for a better school for him," Cade said with an accusing tone.

"Our options are limited here. You know that, and all Phillip talks about is when he's going to be able to go to school. He's twenty-seven, and if he doesn't learn how to be somewhat self-sufficient, then if something happens to me, he's going to rely on you for the rest of his life. Phillip needs to be as independent as possible, and this is his best chance."

"Can I see the school?"

Shirley nodded. "He'll start there in a few weeks. I need to complete some paperwork and then figure out how he's going to get there and back home at first. There is a bus, but they want him to be comfortable, so I'll have to ride with him to start."

"Where is the school?" Cade asked, moving out of Brian's embrace and glaring at his mother.

"It's in the city," was her response, and Cade nodded without softening his eyes. "I need to get him home to bed." Shirley gently woke Phillip and accepted a hug before getting him up. "I appreciate you watching him so much." She gave Brian a smile before she and Phillip left the apartment.

Cade's anger was palpable as soon as the door closed. "What else do you want?" Brian asked. "He's going to be in school, and he'll be in town."

"And what if...?" Cade sputtered and held Brian. "That's just a school where he'll go during the day. It isn't a living center where he can learn to be on his own. It's what's available, but it isn't good enough and not what Phillip needs. You heard him—he wants to be able to have a life of his own, just like you and me, and that's what I want for him too."

"Did Phillip go to school before, when he was younger?"

"Yes. But he had so much trouble keeping up, and even with the special programs, he wasn't able to learn very much. I worked with him for hours so he could try to do well, but he kept getting further and further behind. He wasn't happy, so he didn't respond well."

"Then how did he come as far as he has?"

"Mom and I worked with him a lot, and she fought like a tiger to get him into the best places that could help. But once he turned eighteen, he was out of the system, and Mom found it harder and harder to keep fighting all the time. Now she's going to put him back into another of those schools that he wasn't happy in before. I know he needs help, but I want him to have the best help, not just what's convenient."

Cade rested his head on Brian's shoulder. They stood together, holding one another. Cade seemed wrung out, and Brian slowly moved them toward the bedroom.

"We'll figure something out."

"Brian...."

"Just don't shut me out, okay? I don't know what the answer is at the moment, but we'll figure something out. You need to get some rest so you can think straight." Brian guided Cade to the bathroom. He waited for him on the bed and took his turn to clean up before joining Cade under the covers.

Being close to Cade always made his mind race toward intimacy. He wanted it, and his body reacted when Cade curled close to him, but Brian knew this wasn't the time for sex.

"I'm sorry. I don't feel up to anything tonight."

"I know, and there's nothing to feel sorry about. Things like that happen when I'm around you, and I can't help it." Brian chuckled and tugged Cade a little closer. "You're a special kind of person."

"No, I'm not," Cade argued.

"Yes, you are. You're always thinking of everyone else. You worry about your brother, you helped me, and you try to help your mother as much as you can." Maybe it was time someone took care of Cade.

CHAPTER 9

"YOU'VE BEEN really busy lately," Cade said when he came home from the club. "Since we don't work together anymore, I don't get to see you that often."

Brian had given his notice, and they had enough applicants that Brian was able to pass his job on to someone else in a few days.

"What have you been working on? I know you're up to something because of the way you end your calls whenever I come into the room. Is there something I should know?"

"I have been working on something, but I don't want to tell you what it is, not yet." He didn't want to get Cade's hopes up, but things were coming together very well, almost too well, and he wanted to make sure nothing was going to fall apart. "But I will have something to show you in the next few days." He smiled and pulled Cade into a hug. "This is going to be a good thing. I promise."

"I certainly hope so. You've been so full of energy." Cade smiled sheepishly. "It's been nice, but you're going to wear me out."

Brian chuckled. "I thought we could spend the night at my place if you like." They had been staying most nights at Cade's because... well, to Brian it still felt more like a home than his place did. But tonight he had something special planned, and it was waiting for them. Brian had also checked the work schedule Cade kept in the bedroom, and he knew he was off from both jobs the following day. He had wanted to ask if something strange had happened to give Cade two days off in a row from Bartolome's, but he didn't want to rock the boat.

"Okay. Let me get some of my things. It'll only take a minute." Cade went into the bathroom, and Brian sat on the sofa to wait. He was getting really excited about his project, and he hoped it would make Cade happy. But that wasn't the only reason he was doing it. The more Brian talked to the people involved, the more he realized what he was doing was needed and would be an asset to the community at large. He was doing something good and right, and dang if it didn't feel good.

The photo album still rested on the coffee table, and Brian picked it up, opening to the page with the picture of his mother in her office. "I understand so much more now. You were doing what you thought you had to. It was your dream to help those people, and I understand how that feels now. I hope you'd be proud of me."

When Cade came back into the room, Brian closed the album and put it back into place. Then he joined Cade, and they left the apartment, got into his car, and rode through town to Cudahy Towers.

"What's going on?" Cade asked as they got out, and Brian led him inside the elevator.

He turned and grinned at him. They rode up, and Brian unlocked his condo and motioned Cade inside.

It was exactly as Brian had expected. Nothing had changed. The room was the same he'd always lived in: clean, designer chic, and cold. He felt it now. Everything inside had been expensive, and none of it felt like Cade's small apartment, warm and lived in. It didn't feel like a real home, and Brian had come to realize that it never would.

"I think I'm going to sell this place. I don't need it, and I don't want to live here any longer. I think I want a home, a place with a yard, and for goodness sake, I don't want it too big."

Brian went into the kitchen and opened the refrigerator, pulled out the packages, and placed two in the oven.

"Why?" Cade asked as he wandered over to the windows, staring out. "What's going on down there?"

"That's the Italian Festival. It's this weekend, and tonight is the first night. They used to run Friday through Sunday, but now they added Thursday evening as well. I thought you might want to watch the fireworks."

He set the timer on the oven and walked to where Cade stared out the glass. Brian came up behind him, slid his arms around Cade's waist, and pressed to him, letting his scent surround him.

"Why are you selling this place? It's beautiful."

"This is an address to impress and little more. I don't need to impress anyone any longer, because the only one whose opinion matters and really counts is yours. I was like a peacock, only worried about my tail and the fancy decoration. I thought that would help find me someone perfect. But it wasn't until the tail was taken away and all the fancy trappings gone that I found someone like you."

"It isn't because you're ashamed of me, like what happened at your uncle's party?"

Cade turned slightly, and Brian hummed a negative before gently kissing Cade's neck.

"I'm only proud and amazed by you. With very little, you made a home filled with warmth, where I had everything, and I ended up with a cold condo. You don't just fill your life with warmth—you are the creator of it. You help make your brother feel loved, and you think of him before yourself. I want to try to put you before myself and help take care of you."

"Brian," Cade said with a shiver.

"I know I seem like I'm rushing, and maybe that's one of my faults, of which there are many I'm sure. But this condo isn't my life anymore, and it doesn't represent the kind of life I want."

Cade turned around, and Brian stared into his amazing wide eyes.

"It isn't this."

"You don't need to make all kinds of changes all at once. What if things change once again for you?"

Cade had phrased what he was saying carefully, but Brian saw that Cade wasn't sure Brian's change of outlook was going to last. Hell, if he were honest, he wasn't sure it would last either, so he wanted to make changes to help ensure that it did. He knew if he stayed here and didn't make changes in his surroundings that there was a greater chance he'd slip back into his old habits. They had been with him for years already, after all.

"I want to be a different person," Brian whispered.

"I know you do." Cade moved into his embrace and hugged him.

They stood together at the windows, looking out over the lake, park, and museum below. It wasn't long before the scent of dinner wafted around them, and Cade's stomach growled… loudly.

"Sorry," Cade apologized. "Did you cook?"

"No. I had a friend at Alcazar make up a dish to go." The aromas of rich Middle Eastern spices filled the room, and Brian heard the ding of the timer. "He said all I needed to do was heat it through." Brian released Cade and took his hand. "I need to get the food out of the oven and the table set."

He probably should have done that earlier, but he'd been dashing from appointment to appointment and hadn't had much time. Cade helped him set the glass table for dinner as Brian got the food out of the oven, transferred the cold tabbouleh salad onto plates for each of them, and got the dip into a bowl with pita bread. He opened a bottle of white wine and set everything on the table.

He poured glasses of wine and waited for Cade to take a chair. "I wanted to do something special to say how much I appreciate what you did for me." He sat down and then stood once again to walk around to Cade's side of the table.

"I didn't do much."

Brian bent down and put his arms around Cade's neck, letting his hand rest against his chest. "You were nice to someone whose world had been taken away. I didn't know what was happening and most likely would have had to spend the night in a park or something if you hadn't been kind. I used to think that everything was mine for the taking and that I had everything I could possibly need. But I was missing something really important. Kindness and caring. I was missing you." Brian closed his eyes and rested his head next to Cade's. "I know you have doubts. So do I. But I promised that I'd do my best to show you how I've changed, and I will do exactly that."

"You don't have to prove anything to me." Cade ran his hands up Brian's arms, holding him in return.

"Maybe," Brian whispered. "But if nothing else, I have to prove something to myself."

He did. These changes needed to be here to stay, and Brian needed to make sure he could see what he'd been working on through to the end. It was hard to explain to Cade just how important or nerve-racking what he was doing was and the chance he was taking.

"We should eat dinner, and then in a few hours, it will be time for the fireworks."

Cade turned to look at him. "Whatever will we do in the meantime?"

"Don't worry. I have plans for you."

Brian kissed him with a touch of heat that he hoped promised much for later. Then he returned to his seat, and they had dinner. Brian's mouth burned a little from the intensity of all the spices. The hummus and the cool salad helped take the edge off the rest of the food. It was an amazing blend of hot and cold that kept their palates on edge and seemed to raise the intensity between them. Every time he looked at Cade, the heat built inside his belly. The food was amazing, as he knew it would be, but having it with Cade, especially with the deep moan he made whenever he got a bite of the fruit in the rice dish, sent a zing of heat running through him.

"Your friend makes amazing food," Cade said. "I don't think I've eaten at Alcazar before."

"It's a small place on the east side. He took the building about two years ago and has slowly been building up the place. He has incredible food that isn't going to stay a secret for very much longer."

"Did you go there with your friends?"

Brian shook his head. "I used to go there when I was alone and needed some company. Mutasem is a great guy, and he loves to talk. I'd eat, and we'd talk politics. His family is Palestinian, and they now live in Jordan. His father has a successful business there."

"Then why did he come here?" Cade asked as he emptied his plate.

"He was injured in a camel race and lost an eye. In his culture that meant it was unlikely he'd ever find someone to marry him, so he came over here. Originally his intention was to teach martial arts, but when that didn't work out, he converted the space into a restaurant."

"Did he get married?"

"Yes. He and Claudia have been together a year now, and she's expecting their first child. He's a wonderful man, and he's happy now, but he had a lot of things he needed to get used to." Brian paused. "I know one of those things was me. He's had a difficult time dealing with the gay thing. But I have to give him credit, he's tried very hard to understand, and he's… opened his mind, as he says. I think that's his way of saying live and let live. He also had to get used to American women. Claudia is a strong lady, and I think it took time for him to get his head around having someone in his life like that. She helps him run the business, and some nights she works out front greeting guests. She isn't quiet. I think Mutasem was a little surprised that he fell for her, but I'm glad he did."

"See," Cade said, waving his fork slightly. "You do have other friends, real friends." Cade colored. "I didn't mean that the way it sounded."

"I know what you meant."

"You always said your friends were hangers-on, but it sounds like not all of them were. You just needed to find the rest of them."

Brian nodded slowly. "Maybe. But none of them were around when I needed them." He reached across the table. "That was you, a stranger."

"I have always relied on the kindness of strangers," Cade said, doing his best Blanche DuBois.

"That's definitely my line." Brian grinned. He had relied on Cade's kindness, and it had worked out in ways he never would have imagined.

Brian cleared the table and put the plates and dishes in the dishwasher. He threw away the trash and cleaned up the area where he'd worked before joining Cade in the living room.

"I don't know how you can give up this view." Cade looked at him and then turned to the windows once more. "If you wanted, you could change this place into something warmer and so much homier. Some rugs, get rid of that severe sofa for one that's comfortable to sit on. Maybe a different table, and some color on the walls. You know a place doesn't make a home. It's the person inside that does. So if you want something different in here, then go out and make it different." Cade continued staring.

"It is a great view," Brian agreed, and that view had cost a small fortune. He looked out over the water as the sky slowly darkened. "But there's one that's so much better." Brian shifted his gaze to Cade and waited until he turned to him.

"Brian, when you say things like that, I wonder if they're true."

"Of course it's true. You are a more impressive view than anything out there." He cupped Cade's cheeks in both hands and kissed him, hard. The energy that had been building all through dinner welled up inside him. He feasted on Cade's sweet lips with the hints of spice left from dinner and couldn't possibly get enough. This was the most amazing taste ever.

He let his hands drop lower, tugging at the hem of Cade's gray polo shirt, pulling it upward until Cade lifted his arms and he was able to pull it off. Brian dropped the shirt to the floor and extended his hands, placing the palms flat on Cade's chest, the heat from Cade's skin searing into him. He leaned closer, taking Cade's lips and getting as much intensity as he gave. God, the energy between them was nearly overwhelming, and Brian felt as strong and virile as he ever had in his life. He ended up pressing Cade back against the windowpane, kissing him harder and working open Cade's pants. He needed all of him, right now. There was no way he could stop it. His desire for Cade was nearly overwhelming.

"Brian…." Cade gasped as Brian fumbled with his belt. "Bedroom."

"Huh?" Brian asked as he pressed Cade harder against the window, needing the feel of him. "Sorry." Brian pulled away and took in the sight of him. Cade already looked debauched with his swollen lips, half naked, and his remaining clothes askew. Damn, that was a beautiful sight. He took Cade by the hand, Cade's other keeping his pants up, and he led them to his huge bedroom.

"You could fit my apartment in here." Cade gaped.

"You've seen it before," Brian said.

"Yeah, and I think that every time I come in here." Cade let his jeans fall to the floor and kicked off his shoes and then scrambled out of the jeans, his white-briefed butt waving in the air. "This room could be so amazing with warm colors and…."

Cade seemed intent on decorating, but Brian had other things in mind.

"Stay just like that," Brian whispered and peeled Cade's briefs down over his perfect ass. Amazing—this man was nearly a god, and he didn't know it. For Brian, Cade was perfect. Sure, he had flaws, but Brian didn't notice them, and those he did only made Cade seem even more perfect for him. He rubbed his hands over Cade's backside, stroking his lightly furred rear end.

"What are you—"

Brian bent over Cade, licking down the base of his back and across his butt cheeks before spreading them wide and teasing his puckered skin with his tongue.

"Oh God…," Cade groaned loudly and pressed back against him.

Cade's deep musk drove Brian wild, and he licked harder, rimming Cade and listening to the deep cries that filled the large room. "The sounds you make."

"Me?" Cade moaned. "You're the one doing unspeakable things to me."

Brian helped Cade turn around and felt when he grabbed the edge of the bed. Brian didn't let up, determined to drive Cade absolutely wild. This was incredibly decadent and amazingly sexy. Cade naked and him fully dressed, his cock throbbing in his pants, but he was too busy and too into what he was doing to do anything about it. Cade demanded and deserved his entire attention, and he wasn't going to give Cade a moment's peace until he begged him to stop.

"Brian… I…."

"Hold onto the bed and let me love on you, okay?" All Brian got in response was a whimper, which told him all he needed to know. Brian pressed Cade's legs farther apart, opening Cade fully to him. He stroked gently, slowly down the inside of Cade's legs and then began a slow upward movement, burying his face between Cade's cheeks, feeling him quiver and shake. There was nothing on earth hotter than Cade losing control. It was amazing, incredible, and had Brian on the edge. He had to back off or he was going to come in his pants, and he had plans before that happened.

Brian did back away, breathing deeply as he lifted Cade upward and pressed him onto the bed. Cade bounced on the mattress, looking up at him as Brian pulled off his own shirt and toed off his shoes. He shucked the rest of his clothes quickly and climbed onto the bed. Cade rolled onto his belly, and when Brian knelt on the bed, Cade slid into position and sucked Brian's cock between his lips. He rolled his head back and moaned throatily. Wet heat surrounding him sent him right back to where he'd been before he'd had a few seconds to cool off. Cade had magic lips and applied just the right amount of pressure to drive Brian crazy, but not quite enough to send him over the edge. Brian raised his arms, sliding his fingers through his own hair to hold his head in order to keep it from exploding.

He reached forward, sliding his hands down Cade's back to his bubble butt, massaging the soft skin as Cade continued taking him deeper and driving him higher. Brian wasn't going to last much longer, and this was not how he had envisioned coming.

"I can't.... Is this what you want?" Brian asked, and Cade backed away, rolling onto his back.

"Fuck me, Brian. I want you inside me."

He lifted his legs, and Brian scrambled to grab the supplies and get into position. His ability to think was completely gone now. All that governed him was instinct and the need not to hurt Cade. Everything else was gone, and the entire world had slipped away. It was just him and Cade. He vaguely heard his phone ringing somewhere, but it remained on the edge of his consciousness, and once it stopped, he hardly registered it.

The few moments it took to prepare the condom gave him a chance to cool down from his near-frantic state. But sinking his fingers inside Cade's smooth, tight, blazing passage nearly sent him over once again. "This isn't going to last very long," he warned Cade as he got into position. Brian was already too far gone for much in the way of control.

He nearly shook the bed as Cade's body opened for him. Brian thrummed with so much energy it was hard for him to contain it, and the trust and care in Cade's eyes only added to the intensity. As heat and pressure surrounded him, he had to think unsexy thoughts, and for a second an image of Lydia flashed in his mind. He began to chuckle, but Cade brought him right back to what was important with a soft tap on his thigh.

"You okay?"

Brian thrust forward, burying himself deeply inside Cade, driving away thoughts of anything but him. "Oh yeah. It's just you. No one else but you."

"Brian," Cade gasped and held Brian around his neck. "Are you really sure?"

"Yes. I've been waiting for you for years and didn't know it."

He withdrew and let Cade pull him back inside like a magnet that Brian couldn't resist no matter how hard he tried. Their physical joining was magical, but the spiritual attachment was breath stealing. Cade's eyes glistened. They bored into him so deeply, Brian felt them touch his soul. He didn't want this to end, because when it did, the magic would be gone, but he couldn't stop it no matter how much he tried. What was between them was bigger than Brian, and it had a life of its own.

When the pressure and passion got too much, Brian knew he was going to either burst or lose the ability to stop it. He chose the latter and gave himself over to the magic.

Sweat poured down him in rivulets, and he could barely see. His hips snapped, and Cade's body gripped him tighter and tighter until Cade stilled, coming all over his belly and chest. The sight was more than Brian could stand, and he tumbled into his own release, unable to stop it any longer.

He didn't know what had happened for a few seconds.

"Brian," Cade said.

He opened his eyes. "I think I zoned out for a second."

Cade held him tightly. "You were away for a while. I thought something was wrong."

"No. Nothing, I'm fine."

He held Cade and peppered his face and lips with kisses until Cade stilled him and captured his mouth. Brian had no idea that

Cade could be so dominant, but he refused to let Brian go, and once he turned them on the bed, Cade pressed him into the mattress, holding him still.

"I don't think I have—"

Cade cut him off with a kiss and then placed his head on Brian's shoulder so they could rest.

How long they lay, chest to chest, legs entwined, Brian lost track. And he honestly figured hours could have passed as fast as seconds. Brian groaned when Cade got up and left the room, then returned with a cloth. He laved attention, gentle and firm, over Brian's body before disappearing once again. All Brian could do was blink and wait for Cade to return.

The light in the room faded as darkness fell outside. There were no lights on in the apartment, so the light from outside was all they had.

A flash of red followed blue, and Brian got up, guiding Cade to the window. "This is what I brought you up here for. The Italian Festival has fireworks each night, and I wanted you to see them from here." Brian stood behind Cade, pressed to his back, and they both stood naked at the window watching as the shells burst almost straight ahead of them, some at eye level. It was amazing, and as the shells exploded, their sounds rumbled through the building. They could feel the shock as vibrations that raced through them. It was exciting and dramatic, and it felt as though they were having their own private fireworks that mimicked the ones they'd shared earlier.

"It's beautiful," Cade said, and Brian agreed, only he wasn't looking out the window. He was only looking at Cade.

CHAPTER 10

"WHAT EXACTLY is going on?" Cade asked nearly a week later when Brian met him at his apartment. "Where's your car?"

"At home. Today we don't need it," Brian said as Cade looked up and down the street until a black limousine pulled up in front. "That's our ride now." He opened the door and waited for Cade to get inside.

"What's going on? Does this have something to do with what you've been working on and refusing to say anything about?"

Cade sat down, and Brian closed the door.

"Why did you want me to get dressed up?"

"All will be made clear in just a few minutes," Brian said, taking Cade's hand and trying not to fidget. He was so nervous, and those nerves were not going to help him now. He needed to appear confident and self-assured if he was going to pull this off. The car pulled away from the curb, and Brian sat next to Cade as he looked out the windows.

"Can you at least tell me where we're going?"

"Downtown. To the Paulson offices. For this I wanted home-field advantage." He took Cade's hand and grew quiet as they rode. When the car arrived at the glass high-rise downtown, Brian and Cade got out and instinctively looked upward.

"Brian," Lydia said as she hurried over. "I got your call requesting me to meet you here and that it was important, but what's going on?" She was equal parts perturbed, intrigued, and probably a little off balance.

"It's something I'm going to need your help with." He took her hand. "I think I found what I want to do."

He winked, and Lydia's lips curled upward into a slight smile. He introduced Cade to Lydia then took Cade's hand and led him inside and up to the fifteenth floor. When the doors opened, a number of men in suits turned toward him.

"Thank you all for coming. The conference room is just down the hall." He led the way into what had been his grandfather's private office and motioned everyone to sit.

"You said you had something special you wanted us to see?" the man who had traveled farther than the other men asked.

"Yes, I do." He made sure Cade was comfortable and then turned to everyone. "As you know, Dr. Grantham," Brian continued, addressing the man who had just spoken, "as the head of the UW School for Special Development, your program is the best in the state for adults with learning and developmental difficulties. You and the university have put together an amazing program in Madison, but it can be difficult for some families to relocate there. So I am proposing that we create a facility here in Milwaukee to perform the same function."

"You want me to help create a competing facility?" Dr. Grantham asked.

"No. I want to expand your program to include a facility here in Milwaukee as well, and I want it to have facilities that not only allow the children to stay and learn to function on their own, but I want to include places for families to stay so they can be part of their children's lives when they live out of town." Brian pulled up a cloth that covered an architectural model. "There is a building near the UW Milwaukee campus that has possibilities, and others can be investigated to make sure they are suitable."

"Why are we here?"

"Good question, Mr. Foster. 'Phillip's Dream' is going to cost approximately one hundred million dollars. Rough costs are laid out in the prospectuses on the table. I will be putting up the first forty-nine million dollars of the project. It's the job of the rest of you to secure the funding for the remaining costs. My name will not be on this project or added to the building. This isn't some vanity project but the dream of a friend of mine that I want to see come true."

"The Maxwell Law Firm will undertake all of the legal work for this project at no cost." Lydia looked around the table, her gaze meeting each and every person's. "Brian is continuing Marv's work, and we will all be giving him our support."

"Thank you," Brian said, trying not to get choked up. He had purposely kept his back to Cade because he knew if he looked at him, he wouldn't be able to continue. "There are many details that will need to be finalized, but an architectural firm has already been retained, and as soon as we decide on a location, they will begin drawing up detailed plans under Dr. Grantham's direction." He looked at him and saw Dr. Grantham smiling from ear to ear. "Projects like this can often take time, but we need to get this one moving. There are people who can be served who aren't now. I will lead this project forward with the input and support of those of you who wish to be involved."

"You're expecting a lot," Mr. Foster said.

"My grandfather expected a great deal from each and every one of you, and you delivered or you wouldn't be here. I'm asking that you give me that same support, and in the end we'll be doing a lot of good for people who need a little extra care. I'm proposing a more detailed planning meeting to begin in a week, with finalized commitments from each of you. We'll form a board that I hope you will serve on, and we'll get this project started." Brian turned to Dr. Grantham. "I'll be counting on you to get all of the approvals required of the board of regents."

"Are you kidding?" he asked. "We have wanted to expand the program for years. This is a godsend. When can we see this building you picked out?"

"Whenever you like. We used that building as a planning model, but I'm sure there are plenty we can look at if it doesn't suit." Brian didn't want to get off the track. "Please give this your full consideration."

"I will have someone on my staff act as point person," Lydia said. "Let's throw our support behind it and make this a success."

Lydia was formidable, and Brian had few doubts that he'd won a very powerful ally for the project.

"Are there any further questions? If not, we will be contacting each of you to move forward with the project." Brian waited until each of them stood, shaking hands and greeting them all. He'd seen his grandfather do this on many occasions, and he did exactly as he would have, saying something specific to each person.

Lydia was the last person other than Cade, and Brian was still afraid to look at him. "You're committed to giving away all but the last million," she said with a smile.

"Well, actually, that's something else I wanted to speak with you about. I want to put that in trust for Cade's brother, Phillip. That way he'll always be taken care of and have the support he needs without having to worry." Brian turned to Cade, who had tears running down his cheeks. "If you could set that up for me, I'd really appreciate it. Make Cade, me, and yourself trustees."

"Are you sure you want to give it all away?"

Brian nodded. "I have enough, more than enough for what I need, and if I want more money, I can work for it. I don't think I need to spend the rest of my life living off the work that someone else has done." Brian reached into his pocket and handed Lydia the check she'd given him. "Just make sure the money gets where it's supposed to go." He reached out his hand and felt Cade's slide into his. "Have a good day." He left the office with Cade next to him, and he had never felt better before in his life.

"Why did you do that?" Cade asked as soon as the elevator doors slid closed. "You gave it all away, for Phillip."

"Partially for Phillip, but yes, I did."

161

"Why?" Cade asked once again.

Brian turned to Cade. "The last thing my grandfather asked me to do was find my dream. I got mine already. See, I have the power to make my dreams come true. So do you. Phillip and people like him don't. They rely on other people all their lives. So when I asked Phillip what his dream was and he told me, then I knew that was what I had to do. I don't know how quickly we can make this happen, but I do intend to call the school Phillip's Dream, because that's what it is. My name and the name of my family will not be connected to it. There will be no plaques with donor names attached to it or anything like that." Brian smiled and released the breath he'd been holding.

"So all this was for Phillip, because he told you what his dream was?" Cade asked.

"You could say his dream became my own."

"That was so…." Cade's words trailed off. "I don't know what to say. Other than we owe you a lot."

"No one owes me anything, least of all you." Brian leaned down and kissed Cade in the middle of the lobby with a host of people coming and going around him. Brian didn't care in the least. He truly did have what he always wanted, and that was more than enough. "I fell in love with you a while ago. I'm not sure exactly when, but it happened, and I didn't think I was good enough for you."

"Why would you think that? I'm the one who had nothing."

"The old me would never have given a guy like you a second thought. I was only interested in how things looked, and I acted stupid in order to get people to like me. I should have been myself and found people who liked me for me." Brian held Cade's arm.

"The greatest gift is to be loved for who we are." Cade tugged him closer.

"Isn't that just lovely," Uncle Harry snapped as he walked across the lobby, his voice booming.

"What are you doing here?" Brian asked skeptically. As far as he knew, his uncle never took an interest in any of the business. All he ever seemed to want was the money and prestige that came with it.

"As you know," his uncle said as he paused, haughtiness oozing from every pore, "the majority of the family's assets were put into trust many years ago, and now that Dad has passed, someone needs to head the trust. And since no one seems to have been named, that duty falls to me. I'm on my way to set up a meeting of the trustees to review all of the assets and make sure they are being put to proper use." His uncle strode toward the elevators, and a shiver ran up Brian's spine.

"What?" Cade asked.

"Lord help us all," Brian murmured as he watched his uncle.

When the elevator doors opened, he saw Lydia step out. She approached his uncle, and they spoke for a few minutes. Brian smiled as his uncle's face got redder and redder, and his posture became as rigid as a board. His uncle turned on his heels and strode back across the lobby, passing him and Cade without a single word.

"What was that about?" Cade asked.

"If I had to guess, that was the current head of the family trust popping Uncle Harry's balloon."

"You mean Lydia?" Cade said with a touch of amusement in his smile.

"It makes sense. Grandfather isn't going to let the trust manage itself, and since she's his executor, he'd also make her the head of the trust, at least until things were settled." Brian was becoming more and more impressed with his grandfather. He had truly known his family and thought of everything.

Lydia walked to where he and Cade were standing. "I was wondering if you could come to my office in the morning. I have a few last things I'd like to discuss with you." Lydia shook his hand and then turned to Cade. "I don't know what you and your family did to touch him like this, but it's amazing." Lydia stepped back. "The school is a brilliant idea, and I'm happy to be a part of it."

"I'll see you tomorrow morning," Brian told Lydia, and she hurried away and into a waiting car.

"What do we do now?" Cade asked.

"I don't know. I've been so busy these last few weeks."

"Were you nervous?" Cade asked as they moved toward the door.

"I was, but I think I was more concerned about what you'd think. The rest of those men I could handle. I had the vision and the money to kick-start the project. I was hoping you'd approve of what I was trying to do."

"I do. I can't believe you gave away all that money and that you did it to help Phillip." Cade squeezed his hand. "But the trust fund is too much."

"No, it's not. Phillip is going to need support and care for the rest of his life, and with it maybe he'll be able to dream a little. You and I can dream on our own, but he is going to need some help." He had some other ideas to help Phillip, but he wasn't going to bring them up now. Those could come about in time.

"I have to say that when you dream, you do it big."

They approached the limousine. The driver opened the door, and they climbed inside. Brian sat back on the seat with a smile on his face. At that very moment he had a purpose in life and someone he cared very deeply about. Life was really good, and he was happier than he'd been in a very long time.

Brian put an arm around Cade's shoulders and held him close. As the driver pulled away, he wondered if this was how life should be.

"I wonder what Lydia wants tomorrow," Cade asked as he rested his head lightly on Brian's shoulder.

"It doesn't really matter. I get what my grandfather was trying to say with all this, and I'm not going back to the way things were."

"Have you forgiven him?" Cade asked, shifting so they could look at each other.

"Yes. I still wish things had been different, but he had his life to lead, and he made his choices. They weren't always perfect, but I know he cared about me. He just wasn't sure how to show it."

"It could be that the grief over losing your mother was more than he could stand and that you were a reminder of that grief. Then he lost your grandmother and pretty much withdrew." Cade was always good at getting to the emotions behind things.

It was a possibility, but Brian wasn't as concerned with what was behind it. The past was the past, and he had his entire future ahead of him. One he hoped would include Cade.

"So where are we going?"

"I thought we could go to my place." Brian began to fidget a little.

"Are you overthinking again?" Cade asked.

Brian always seemed to do that when he wasn't sure of something. It was amazing how Cade could read him.

"Maybe a little. I know you like the view from there, so I was wondering if you might consider living with me someday. I was going to sell the place and see about getting something different, but you really like the view, so I was going to look into redecorating, and maybe you could help with that." He hadn't been this nervous when he'd been standing in front of those important people to present his proposal. He knew it was because Cade was the most important person of all. "I want a home, and I want my place to feel like a home. For weeks I've thought of your apartment as homier than anywhere I've lived as an adult, and I realize that it's because you were there."

"Brian… it's a little early to talk about things like that."

"Probably, and I shouldn't have brought it up."

He hoped he hadn't messed things up, but Cade's smile told him things were fine.

"Let's take things one step at a time. I know we were living together for a while and we've been sleeping together for some weeks now. I just don't want to…. I don't know. But I feel that when we make a commitment, it should be permanent." Cade leaned over, the seat crinkling slightly as he moved. "We have time to see how everything will work. Let me think about it for a little while."

"We don't have to make any decisions right away." Brian was content. He hadn't expected Cade to say yes and to start moving in, but Cade also hadn't shut down the idea altogether.

After a few more minutes, they pulled up in front of Cudahy Tower and got out of the limousine. "Do you have another of those gourmet takeaway meals waiting for us?" Cade asked.

"No. I thought I'd try cooking for us. It'll be simple, but I wanted to try making something on my own." He put his arm around Cade's waist, and they walked inside and went up to his floor for a celebration for just the two of them.

CHAPTER 11

BRIAN WAS shown into the conference room in Lydia's law office the following morning. Cade had had to go into work, but Brian wished he was here with him. They'd had an incredible night, but being back here brought out doubts he'd rather not have.

"I know you're wondering why I asked you here," Lydia said as she took the seat next to his.

"I thought this was over," Brian said quietly.

"You'll find out that very few things are over when we think they are." Lydia turned the chair to face him. "I have one final message from your grandfather." She pressed the button on the remote.

"Brian, if you're listening to this message, then you've completed all of the things I hoped you would, and you made some hard decisions. This message was to be played only in the event that you did something worthwhile and meaningful with the money I left you. What I hope more than anything is that you now understand the inner satisfaction that comes from helping others. It's very easy for any of us to put ourselves first, but once we have more than we could possibly need, it's my feeling that we must help others so that they can reach their dreams."

"I tried to," Brian muttered without thinking. The man on the screen wasn't like the others in the previous messages. He seemed to still have some of the energy that Brian remembered, as though this message was made first.

"What I gave you before was not your true inheritance, or at least I hoped it wouldn't be."

The message paused, and Brian turned to Lydia.

"Your grandfather made almost two dozen messages for you, a few of which you haven't seen and I will send home with you. Others will be destroyed because they weren't needed. Those were the instructions I was given. This is the one message he most hoped you would be able to hear."

She returned her attention he the screen, and Brian followed her gaze.

"Your inheritance isn't so much a check or a business as a job. This is one that I hope you will be able to take on and continue for a very long time. As you know, many of our family's assets have been placed in trust to support the family as it grows and to ensure that our family continues to work for the benefit of others as I hoped. I held the title of chairman of the trust committee and was the chief trustee. I am leaving that job to you, Brian, along with the remainder of my personal assets."

Lydia paused the recording, and Brian turned to gaze at her. "Me? Good Lord," Brian whispered.

"Your grandfather's remaining personal assets are estimated at nearly a half billion dollars, and the trust manages assets worth nearly two billion."

Brian began to shake as the weight of responsibility settled onto his shoulders. "What if I completely mess everything up?"

Lydia picked up the phone and spoke softly into it. Then she hung up, and the conference room door opened, with Emily leading Cade inside.

"Thank you for coming," Lydia told him as she stood and motioned to the chair next to Brian.

"I don't know why I'm here. This is about Brian," Cade said as he took the seat, and Brian held his hand.

He needed someone at his side right about now, and he was happy Lydia understood that.

"I thought you both should hear this part of his message," she said and sat back down.

"Brian, you're my grandson, and I love you very much. But I know your affections do not run the same as mine. You aren't attracted to women, and that's fine. You are who you are, and that's perfectly okay."

Brian turned to Lydia. "He knew? I can't believe my grandfather knew all this time and he…. I…." Brian realized he'd missed out on an opportunity to have been closer to his grandfather if he'd simply opened up to him. "I was such a fool."

"You and your grandfather were both hurting for different reasons. He could have approached you as well," Cade said gently. "It doesn't do you any good to beat yourself up. You forgave him, and this is his way of saying that he tried to understand. It isn't something to get angry about."

"How did you get so smart about these things?" Brian asked, turning to Cade and bringing his hand to his lips.

"One of us has to be," Cade said, and Brian rolled his eyes but didn't argue.

"Your grandmother was the light of my life," his grandfather continued, and Brian returned his attention to the screen. "I could never have done any of the things I was able to accomplish without her. She was always there to support and care for me and our family. Brian, I can't tell you how important it is for you to find someone who will be that support and partner through life. I haven't given you the easiest road. Managing the trust, and by extension the family, will not be an easy task, but it's one I hope you won't undertake alone."

Brian squeezed Cade's hand as he saw Cade's mouth hang open.

"The best things in life are better when they're shared, and the hardest of challenges is eased when you aren't alone to face it."

"I've learned that," Brian muttered.

"You also have to know who your real friends are and cultivate people you know you can trust. Lydia is one such person, as are a number of my associates. I hired good people who can handle responsibility. However, you will need to build your own circle of people that you trust, and all that starts with the one you love most. When you find him, cherish and hold onto him the way I did your grandmother. Losing her was like losing a part of me, but I wouldn't give up a single thing, not even the loss, because of all the amazing years we had together."

Brian was silent, just holding Cade's hand, almost immobile.

"Brian, there is just one last thing I want you to know. I loved your mother dearly, she was precious to me, and when I lost her and your grandmother, it nearly killed me. But that doesn't mean I ever stopped loving you. I lost my way for quite a while and focused solely on my work rather than on what was truly important. In the end I found my way back, but it was too late."

Tears ran down Brian's cheeks. "It didn't have to be too late."

"I want nothing but happiness for you. I want you to know that. I love you, Brian."

The image of his grandfather stilled, and then his face faded away as the screen went blank.

Brian sat still, almost unable to process all that he'd been told in the last few minutes. Cade held his hand, and Brian kept watching the screen, his eyes sheened over, hoping for more, for one last glimpse of his grandfather. "I wish I'd known then…."

"He understood that," Cade said. "That's why he did all this."

"Cade's right. Marv wasn't sure how to say what he wanted to, and in the end he felt the gulf might have gotten too wide."

"So he devised all this to do what he could have done by coming over, sitting down, and just talking to me?" Brian asked.

Lydia didn't have the answer. She pursed her lips slightly.

"Things are never that easy. You know that. If he had come over, would you have listened?" Cade asked, and Brian knew he was probably correct. Brian had long held ideas of what was fact, and now those notions had been challenged on so many fronts.

"Maybe not. But why did he do this?"

"Your grandfather still had faith in you, and you proved that his faith was correct." Lydia stood and extended her hand. "You know I'm here if you ever need anything."

Brian stood as well. "I know, and I appreciate all your advice." He shook her hand and then turned to Cade. Everything had changed in a few hours. Last night he thought he had all he could have wanted—Cade and a life he could build for the two of them—and he'd been happy. Now, within hours, responsibility was settling on him like a heavy weight, and yet Cade was still there, holding his hand tightly like he had no intention of letting go.

"Thank you," Cade told Lydia.

She nodded and waited as they left the conference room. Now it was Cade's turn to lead him to the elevator, and they rode down to the street.

"Let's go home." Cade walked with Brian to his car.

"Where do you want to go? My place, yours?" He wasn't sure exactly what Cade meant by home.

"Haven't you figured it out yet? That doesn't matter. Wherever you and I are together, that's home." Cade stopped him on the street, turned to him, and wrapped his arms around Brian's neck, kissing him right there. "Now take me home. We have a lot to talk about."

Cade turned, and they got into the car. Brian stopped to look at Cade, with his magic blue eyes and bright smile, and the load on his shoulders lightened.

"CADE," BRIAN said when they entered the door of his apartment. "This is too much." The entire drive he had been trying to figure out how he was going to manage everything that his grandfather had just laid on his shoulders. A ton of responsibility had thunked down on him in a matter of minutes.

"No, it's not. It's what you were born for, and you'll be good at it."

He took Brian's hand and led him over to the windows. They stood quietly, looking out at the lake.

"You don't have to do this alone. There are other trustees and people your grandfather trusted. Over time you'll learn who you can trust, and you'll build your own circle of advisors."

"That's what worries me. I know Grandpa had good instincts, but mine are severely compromised." Brian thought back to the friends who had deserted him.

"I don't think so. This douche Peter from the gym, you know he's going to call as soon as the word gets out that you've inherited. He'll want to go out again and try to worm his way into your good graces, even after turning his back and acting like a spoiled brat. What are you going to do?" Cade cocked a single eyebrow expectantly.

"Peter is no friend of mine. I thought he was, but… that's what I'm worried about. I thought a lot of people were, and look what happened."

"That's the point. Now you know, and when those people show up again…." Cade placed his hands on his hips.

"They'll get nowhere and a polite brushing off," Brian said.

"Polite?" Cade asked smugly. "You can let me handle them, and I'll tell them where they can take a long walk off a very short pier." Cade's eyes were dark with anger. "You're a good man, Brian, but you let people get the better of you because you wanted to be liked."

"Maybe," Brian said. He was willing to concede that.

"But you are liked. I like you." Cade took Brian's hand. "Phillip likes you, and if you were really the self-centered egotist you played before this began, he wouldn't have anything to do with you. Phillip has a great sense for people."

"Maybe I can bring him into business meetings with me," Brian quipped.

"I know you're kidding, but you know Phillip would love that, and he'd charm every single person in that room." Cade smiled, and Brian felt a little better. "You'll learn. You know that. And you have Lydia. You trust her, don't you?"

"Yes."

"Then let her be your barometer until you develop one yourself. There are people you already know who are going to have their own agenda."

"Yeah, my aunt and uncle." God, he could only wonder what they would say and how they'd react once they heard. Not that it mattered. Lydia would stand with him, and there wasn't much either of them could do to stand against her. She was formidable. "Thanks, Cade," Brian whispered. "I feel better."

"Like I said, you aren't alone." He moved closer. "But never ask me to be on one of those boards or to manage any part of the estate for you. That isn't what I want. That money and everything that comes with it is your business, not mine." He squeezed Brian's hand. "I want you to know, and never doubt, that I'm here and with you because of you. Not the money or anything that comes with it. I'll help manage the trust you set up for Phillip, but that's all. I'll be here for you, support you, and care for you without doubt, because I love you. But that money isn't mine, and I don't want it. I want you, and I never want you to doubt that."

"I don't," Brian said right away. That was the one thing he was sure of. Cade had been shocked when Brian told Lydia and him about his plans for a trust for Phillip and what he planned to do with the money. When he had eventually chanced a look at Cade, all he'd seen was pride and happiness. He realized now that yesterday had been a test for Cade. Not that Brian had meant it that way, but in hindsight it told him a lot that Cade hadn't gotten angry that he'd given the fifty million away.

Brian guided Cade's lips to his, kissing him gently. Knowing he had a partner who would support him through the difficulties ahead made the road he was going to have to walk bearable.

"I can do this," he whispered.

"Of course you can. You're Brian Paulson, and you can do anything. You're strong and smart, and you have a good heart when you keep it engaged. That will take you far. I have every confidence in you."

The sincerity in Cade's voice reached all the way to Brian's heart, and he hugged Cade tightly. Maybe he could do anything if he had Cade by his side.

Brian guided Cade away from the window and through the condo to the bedroom, where they ended up tumbling onto the bed. Cade laughed, and Brian joined him until the joy was cut off by a kiss that deepened and heated quickly. Passion replaced mirth, and they divested themselves of their clothing. He needed Cade next to him, to feel him and know he was real. It seemed like a strange notion, but with all that had happened, he needed to feel grounded. Cade did that for him—well, in a way. Cade's body and heat grounded him, and yet his touch and the way he kissed him made his heart soar and showed him that anything was possible. Even something as unlikely as a wonderful person like Cade actually loving him.

He feasted on Cade's lips, their tongues dueling as Brian cupped Cade's butt in his hands. This was happiness, and it was all he really needed.

"What is it?" Cade asked.

Brian hadn't realized he'd stilled and was staring at nothing. "This is all I need. You. I always kept looking outward to try to find what would make me happy. My mother, my grandfather… and everyone. I always expected them to make me happy, and they disappointed me. Everyone did."

"Brian, it happens," Cade said as he pressed closer, his warmth surrounding him.

"Maybe, but it was my fault, not theirs. They were being themselves, and I expected more from them than they were willing to give. I expected them to make me happy, even after I grew up and should have known better."

"I don't understand, and Brian—" He glanced downward. "—is the time to have this conversation really when you have your hands on my bare ass?"

"Maybe not, but I get it now. Being happy comes from inside me. And I am happy—you make me happy, not because of what you do, but because of who you are and what you mean to me. I know things won't always work out, but we can get through anything together." He knew that in his heart.

Cade kissed him, his lips soft, and soon the heat between them built once again until Brian's thoughts centered only on where Cade's lips sucked at his and then down his neck. When Cade built the heat further, sliding down his body and then taking him in one wet, heated glide, Brian figured he could give up thinking for the rest of his life. He arched his back, pressing for more, and Cade bobbed his head, sucking him perfectly... and the way he used his tongue.... Brian swallowed hard and lifted his gaze just so he could watch Cade take him.

"Love how you do that."

Cade let him slip from his lips and brought their mouths together once again. "I know. You're like an open book to me. You stopped hiding, and those walls you built up are gone, at least around me."

Cade pressed him into the mattress, and Brian groaned and wrapped his legs around Cade's waist. He had never allowed himself to be vulnerable with anyone, but he trusted Cade and was willing... no, *wanted* to give himself to him. Cade wouldn't hurt him or play games. Cade was his, and he belonged to Cade. His heart and body were safe in Cade's hands. And he proved it by using his fingers to send Brian to tongue-tying, throat-drying heights that left him on the edge but never tumbling over. Cade waited until he pressed his enrobed cock to Brian's entrance and silently held his gaze, asking final permission, before Brian nodded, and Cade slowly pressed into him, joining them together, making Brian soar, pant, and cry until neither of them could hold back any longer.

"You make me happier than I ever thought possible," Brian whispered later when Cade rested in his arms.

"I love you too," Cade told him as he rolled onto his side and held Brian a little tighter.

EPILOGUE

Early December

"BRIAN, ARE you sure about this?" Cade asked as he came out of their bedroom and into the living room. What had been Brian's condo—which was now his and Cade's home—had changed a great deal. The severe glass-and-chrome dining table and chairs had been replaced with a set they'd found together when they'd gone to Chicago for a weekend. The rug under it had also changed to one they'd found at an auction in the early fall. The living room chairs were now large and comfortable masculine leather around a deep red oriental rug. They were using Cade's end tables for now until they found ones they liked better, and the walls were decorated with pictures of their families, including some of the prints from the photo album that Cade had had duplicated and framed. In short, Brian's condo felt like a home, and he had given up the notion of selling it. Cade loved the view and he loved Cade, so they stayed. Maria helped take care of the house and both of them, and Brian had come to realize she was much more than a housekeeper.

"We have the extra bedroom," Brian told him.

"But what about when I'm at work?" Cade asked.

Brian ground his teeth. He had been trying to convince Cade to stop working at Bartolome's and go back to school or whatever he wanted, but he understood Cade's need for independence. "I'll be here part of the time, and I can create a space in my office if necessary." Brian was more certain about this than he was about most things.

"But Brian," Cade said as he came closer. "Phillip will need someone to care for him."

"Sweetheart," Brian said, tugging Cade down onto the sofa. "What's the real problem? Your mother's health isn't going to allow her to take care of Phillip like she has been."

She had been rediagnosed with cancer in the early fall and was fighting it with all she had, but up till a few weeks ago, the cancer had been winning.

"She needs to know that Phillip has a home long-term, and you know the best place for him is with us. He'll go to his new school once the project is finished, and until then his caregiver will come in during the week, and we'll work things out."

Cade pressed his head to Brian's shoulder. "You're really serious about this?"

"Yes, I am. I was thinking that if it works out, maybe we could see about getting him a job. One that he could do. That is, when he's ready."

Cade lifted his head away and caught Brian's gaze. "I love you for this. Well, I love you more for this."

There had never been any doubt in Brian's mind that when Shirley became ill, they would open their home to Phillip. He already had a space for when he came to stay. They'd only make it more permanent for him.

"I'm more worried about how your mother is going to feel once he moves in here," Brian explained.

"I think Mom needs to rest for a while. She's lived for Phillip and me for many years. It's time she got a chance to live for herself a little. And it isn't like she won't see him." Cade's anxiety seemed to be waning.

"Good."

Brian hugged Cade close and was figuring that things could get a little heated when his phone rang. Brian huffed and ignored it, but Cade picked it up and showed him the screen. He saw Lydia's name and took the phone.

"Do you have good news?"

"You sound just like Marv," Lydia said. "I called for two reasons. First, I'd be honored to attend your Christmas party, and Emily says she's looking forward to it as well." Her smile was evident in her voice. "I also called with some news. The suit your aunt and uncle filed to contest the will is falling apart fast. Their grounds got shakier when I made the judge aware of your uncle's political aspirations. It seems he wasn't convinced that your uncle wouldn't use the funds to finance his campaign rather than for the stated purpose of the family trust."

"Okay," Brian said with a smile.

"His claim was spurious at best, and the will is sound. I can prove that in Marv's own words. So I suspect this whole thing will be over very soon, and there will be nothing to worry about." She sounded happy. "Just a minute," she said and put him on hold.

"My aunt and uncle's lawsuit is coming apart." Brian smiled, and Cade nodded.

"Those two are looney tunes," Cade said, and Brian chuckled in agreement. His aunt and uncle had been livid beyond words when Brian explained his new role and expressed his view and that of the other trustees that their services were no longer needed or required. Lydia had suggested it in order to keep the trust from getting bogged down in family infighting.

"I'm sorry for the interruption, Brian. I just received word that the purchase of the property for Phillip's Dream has been completed, and after the committee approves the plans, we can move forward. I think an early spring groundbreaking would be perfect."

Things had taken longer than he hoped, but that the project was moving forward was great news.

"That's great." He grinned. "I have an idea for another I'd like to start, but it can wait until after Christmas. I'll see you at the party." He hung up and told Cade all the news.

"It's going to be a wonderful gathering," Cade said, and they returned to what they'd been doing.

TWO WEEKS later the condo was decorated to the hilt, and Phillip sat excitedly, staring at the tree positioned right in front of the windows. "Will they be here soon?" Phillip asked, dressed in dress pants and a shirt that Cade had bought him. Phillip kept pulling at the collar, and Brian walked over to him to take a look.

"You need to take the plastic out," Brian said, removing the packaging, and Phillip sighed and was instantly much more comfortable. "Now, if you get tired, it's okay to go to your room and lie down."

"I know I can go to bed, and Cade said he would be sure to tell me good night, and not to come out in my pajamas."

"Very good." Brian smiled and gave his brother a hug. Phillip had christened him his other brother shortly after moving in, and Brian was tickled with the designation. "You understand your job for tonight?"

"To smile and be charming," Phillip said with a grin that would disarm Russia.

"That's right. Have fun." Brian turned away as Cade came into the room wearing black pants and a royal blue shirt that set off his eyes. Brian's attention focused on him instantly.

"What?" Cade asked, looking down at his clothes.

"You look very handsome." Brian hurried over and scooped Cade into his arms, kissing him as the doorbell rang. The first of their guests were arriving.

A steady stream of people followed, and within an hour the apartment was filled with holiday cheer and overlapping conversation and laughter. Garrett, his former boss from the gym, had come with his girlfriend, as had some of the people Cade worked with. The committee members for Phillip's Dream were all there, as were other associates and friends.

"Courtney," Cade called when he saw her arrive.

He wove his way over with Brian in tow. She grinned, and they hugged and rocked back and forth with excitement. Cade looked at her date for the evening.

"I see you took my advice."

"He proposed," Courtney squealed giddily and flashed her ring. Kyle stood next to her, beaming.

"That's awesome," Cade said, admiring the bling on her finger while Brian shook hands with her fiancé.

"She's amazing," Kyle said, still grinning.

"That she is, and you're both very lucky."

In so many ways. Not least of all to have had a friend like Cade who cared enough to get them together. Kyle puffed up and looped Courtney's arm through his.

"He's so nice," Courtney was saying to Cade as Brian returned his attention to his partner. "And he treats me like a lady."

"You always were, honey," Cade told her. "You just forgot for a while." She and Cade hugged again, and then Cade moved off with them to show them where everything was.

Lydia came with her husband and oldest grandson, who seemed to hit it off with Phillip, and they disappeared into Phillip's room to play games for much of the evening.

"Do you miss them?" Lydia asked as she joined Brian near the tree as he took a breather from near constant conversation.

"Who?"

"Your old friends." She handed him a glass of champagne.

"I really thought they were my friends, and I do miss them sometimes, but I have so much more now." He turned to where Cade stood talking with a group of bankers, and from the smile on Cade's face, he knew they weren't talking finance. Most likely food. Maybe he should convince Cade to open a restaurant if he wanted. "But I do miss them sometimes. I went out with a few of them a week ago, and it was tedious and dull."

"Why'd you go?"

"To see if there was anything there. It showed me that I'd changed and they hadn't. In the end I paid the bill and left. I won't attempt contact again." It had been disappointing.

"I don't see your aunt and uncle or any other of your family."

"That was another lesson as well. I may have been born a Paulson, but the family that counts is the one you create for yourself."

He raised his glass, and Lydia lightly clinked it in a silent toast. They each drank, and Lydia put her hand on his shoulder.

"I don't usually say this, but seeing their lawsuit die around them was an amazing sight." She looked around the room at the gathering as Cade walked over to join them. "Your grandfather had an amazing ability to read people, and that extended all the way up to you."

"I hope I don't let him down," Brian said as he put an arm around Cade's waist.

"I doubt that's possible." She took another sip from her glass and moved away.

Brian caught Cade's eye, and they stared at each other for a few seconds. Then Cade turned away and tinked his glass.

Cade cleared his throat. "If I could have your attention for just a moment."

The room grew quiet, and Cade continued. "This year has been one of changes, lots of changes for both Brian and me. Each of you has had a part in those changes, and Brian and I want to thank you all for your friendship and support throughout the year. Merry Christmas, and here's to more amazing changes and challenges to come."

"Hear, hear," echoed through the room as glasses clinked together.

Brian turned to Cade and leaned in close.

"To the biggest and best change of all," Brian said, and Cade leaned in close and kissed him.

ANDREW GREY grew up in western Michigan with a father who loved to tell stories and a mother who loved to read them. Since then he has lived all over the country and traveled throughout the world. He has a master's degree from the University of Wisconsin-Milwaukee and now works full-time on his writing. Andrew's hobbies include collecting antiques, gardening, and leaving his dirty dishes anywhere but in the sink (particularly when writing). He considers himself blessed with an accepting family, fantastic friends, and the world's most supportive and loving husband. Andrew currently lives in beautiful historic Carlisle, Pennsylvania.

E-mail: andrewgrey@comcast.net
Website: www.andrewgreybooks.com

FIRE AND Snow

ANDREW GREY

Carlisle Cops: Book Four

Fisher Moreland has been cast out of his family because they can no longer deal with his issues. Fisher is bipolar and living day to day, trying to manage his condition, but he hasn't always had much control over his life and has self-medicated with whatever he could find.

JD Burnside has been cut off from his family because of a scandal back home. He moved to Carlisle but brought his Southern charm and warmth along with him. When he sees Fisher on a park bench on a winter's night, he invites Fisher to join him and his friends for a late-night meal.

At first Fisher doesn't know what to make of JD, but he slowly comes out of his shell. And when Fisher's job is threatened because of a fire, JD's support and care is more than Fisher ever thought he could expect. But when people from Fisher's past turn up in town at the center of a resurgent drug epidemic, Fisher knows they could very well sabotage his budding relationship with JD.

www.dreamspinnerpress.com

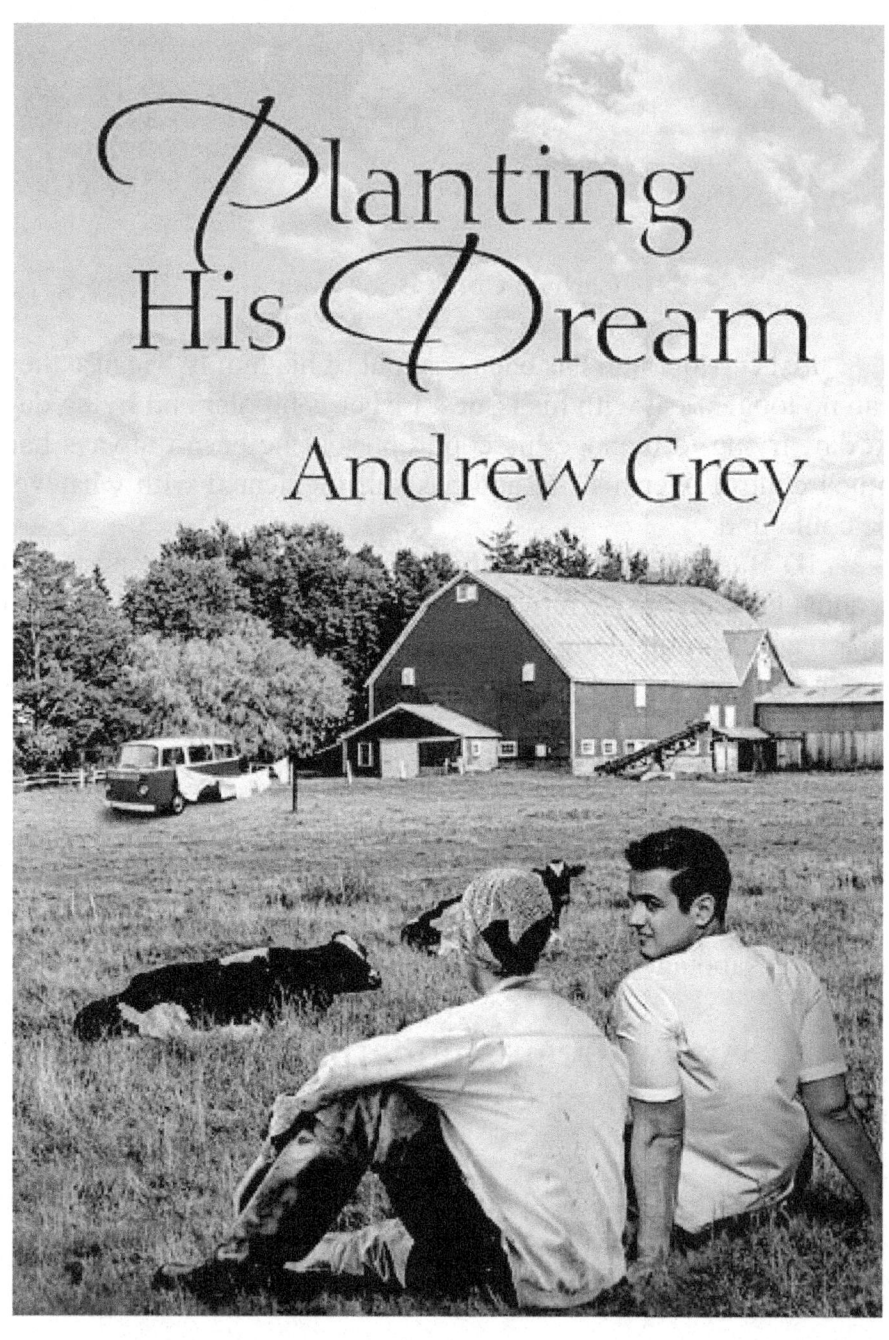

Planting His Dream

Andrew Grey

Foster dreams of getting away, but after his father's death, he has to take over the family dairy farm. It soon becomes clear his father hasn't been doing the best job of running it, so not only does Foster need to take over the day-to-day operations, he also needs to find new ways of bringing in revenue.

Javi has no time to dream. He and his family are migrant workers, and daily survival is a struggle, so they travel to anywhere they can get work. When they arrive in their old van, Foster arranges for Javi to help him on the farm.

To Javi's surprise, Foster listens to his ideas and actually puts them into action. Over days that turn into weeks, they grow to like and then care for each other, but they come from two very different worlds, and they both have responsibilities to their families that neither can walk away from. Is it possible for them to discover a dream they can share? Perhaps they can plant their own and nurture it together to see it grow, if their different backgrounds don't separate them forever.

www.dreamspinnerpress.com

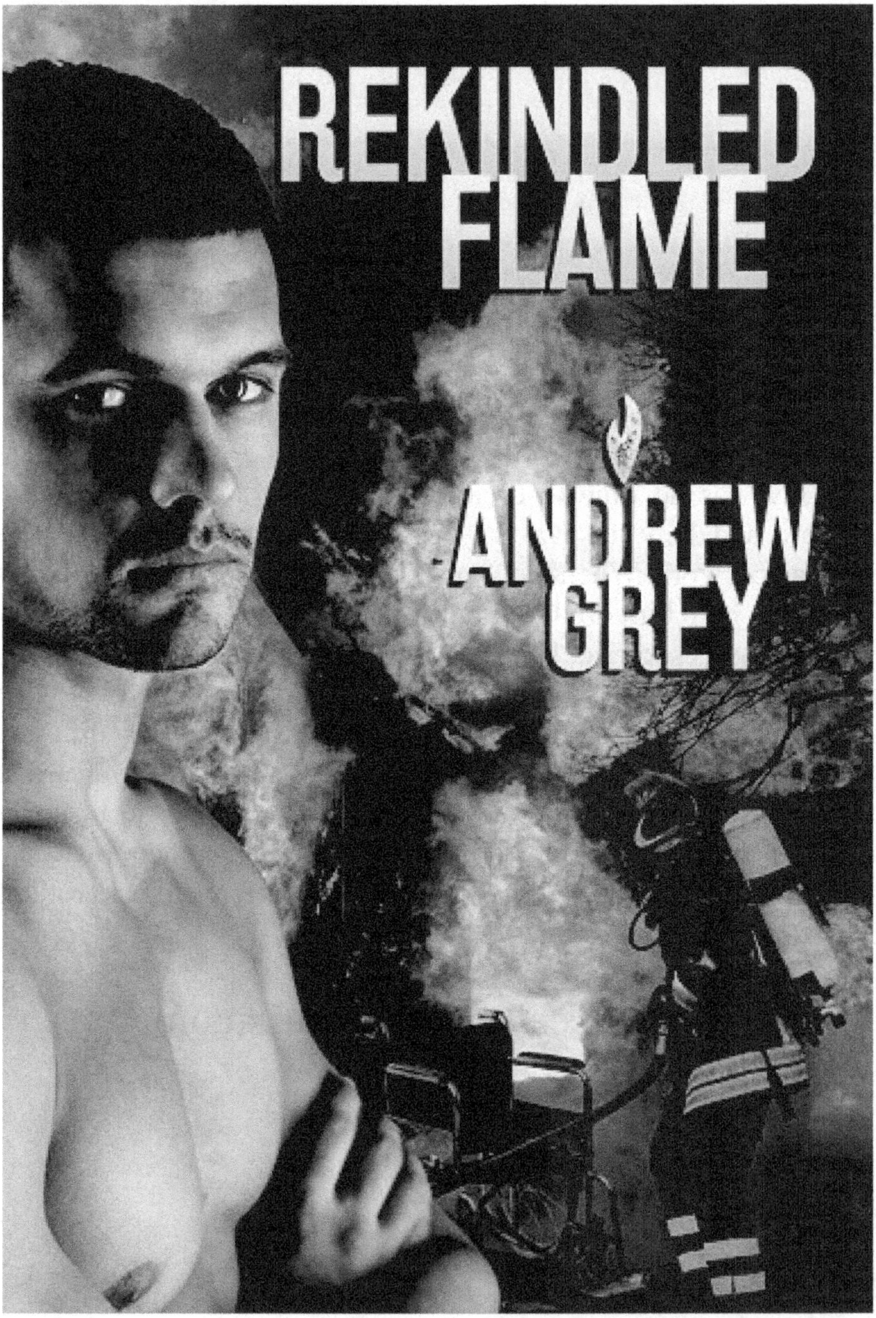
REKINDLED
FLAME
ANDREW
GREY

Firefighter Morgan has worked hard to build a home for himself after a nomadic childhood. When Morgan is called to a fire, he finds the family out front, but their tenant still inside. He rescues Richard Smalley, who turns out to be an old friend he hasn't seen in years and the one person he regretted leaving behind.

Richard has had a hard life. He served in the military, where he lost the use of his legs, and has been struggling to make his way since coming home. Now that he no longer has a place to live, Morgan takes him in, but when someone attempts to set fire to Morgan's house, they both become suspicious and wonder what's going on.

Years ago Morgan was gutted when he moved away, leaving Richard behind, so he's happy to pick things up where they left off. But now that Richard seems to be the target of an arsonist, he may not be the safest person to be around.

www.dreamspinnerpress.com

Made in United States
Orlando, FL
22 March 2026

79559312R00115